ARI ROSENSCHEIN

Coasting

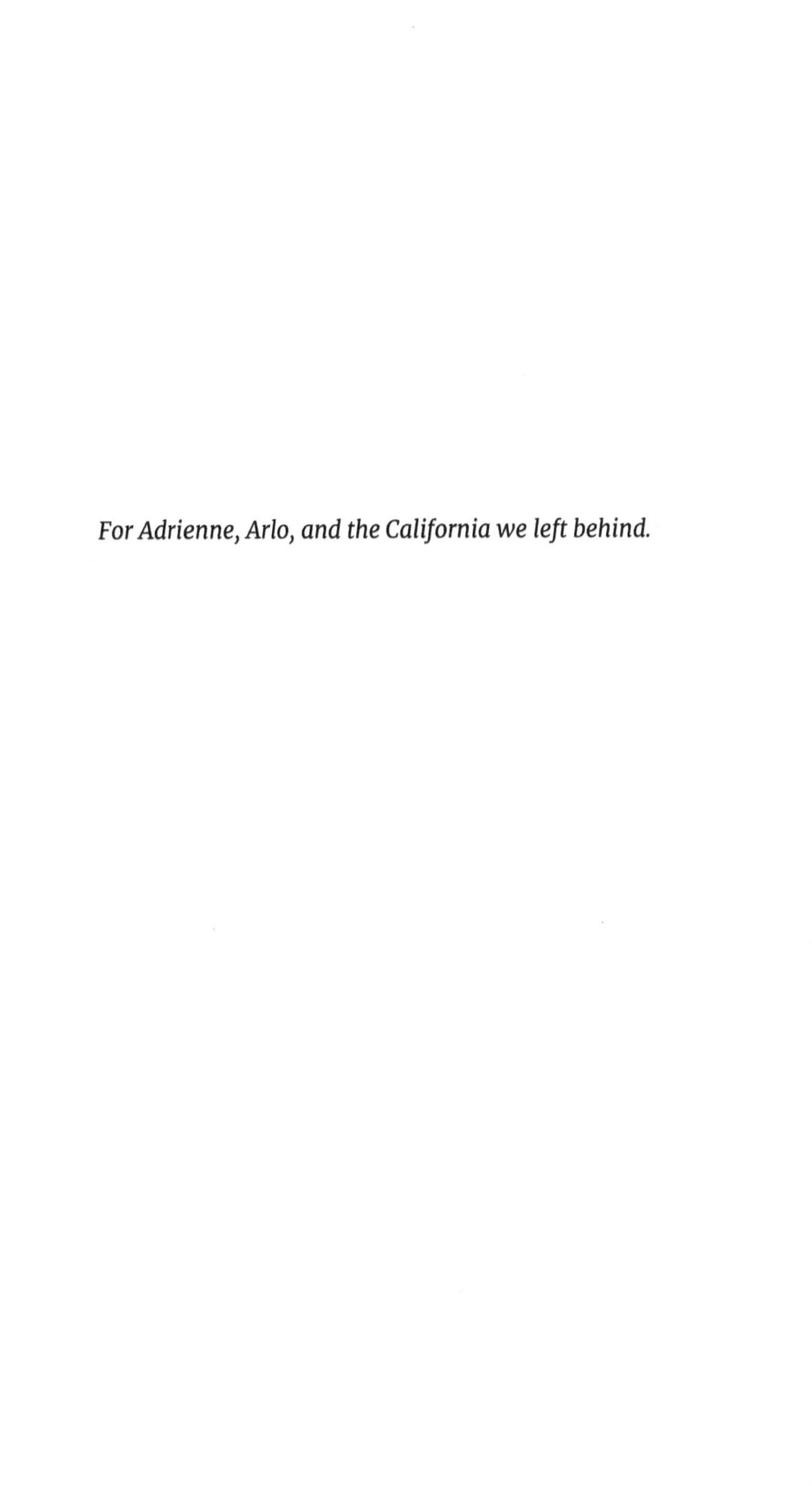

For Adrienne, Arlo, and the California we left behind.

Contents

Praise for Coasting

"With the insight of a socio-anthropologist and the familiarity of your favorite bartender, Ari Rosenschein introduces us to new West Coast archetypes who follow the tradition of California Dreaming into the twenty-first century."
—**Nikki San Pedro**, *Newfound Journal*

"Ari Rosenschein's *Coasting* is a unique, funny, and unsettling story collection, populated with hipsters, drifters, dreamers, band members, and insiders who feel like outsiders. With sharp prose and intimate details, *Coasting* reveals a Los Angeles full of grief, loss, disappointment, illusions, and especially surprise."
—**Victoria Patterson**, author of *The Secret Habit of Sorrow* and *The Little Brother*

"Ari Rosenschein's *Coasting* does for Gen Y punks and rockers seeking artistic fame and glory in Los Angeles roughly what Candide did for—and to—its naïvely optimistic protagonist. A superb debut collection."
—**Peter Selgin**, author of *Duplicity* and *Life Goes to the Movies*

"Ari Rosenschein's *Coasting* is not only quick, it's quick-witted and razor sharp and not without its fair share of knowing nods and chuckles at the ridiculousness of, in general, the lives we lead when we're trying to convince ourselves of their greater significance. A must-read."

—**Eugene Robinson**, author of *Fight: Everything You Ever Wanted to Know About Ass-Kicking but Were Afraid You'd Get Your Ass Kicked for Asking*

"*Coasting* captures the infectious buzz of aspiration and the omnipresent pall of rejection, the too-bright October sun, the smell of cigarettes and strawberry lip gloss, losing your live-show virginity, getting the wrong tattoo, hiring the wrong drummer, falling for the wrong girl or the wrong scam, or all of it, all at once, and still taking it all in stride. Rosenschein's writing brims with tenderness for the last holdouts in a city of seekers and real passion for books, games, comics, and music, always music, every kind of music. His characters inhabit a backstage space, a few steps from glory, looking for the next gig, hoping for a big break, reveling in every note along the way. Their sweet, gritty persistence is irresistible."

—**Ana Maria Spagna**, author of *Uplake: Restless Essays of Coming and Going*

"Punk rock, love and sex, petty theft, and hawking guitars to pay the rent—Ari Rosenschein's breakout collection of stories, *Coasting*, is a true-to-life rendition of the everyday misfortunes of misfit musicians trying to make it big in Tinseltown. Candid, poignantly tragic, and humorous, Rosenschein's stories pluck at the nitty-gritty of what it takes to coast. The anxiety and thrill will keep you turning pages."

—**Sarah Jones**, author of *Lies I Tell Myself*

"The neighborhoods, restaurants, venues, bands, and pop culture references that permeate *Coasting*—Los Feliz, Sunset,

Intelligentsia, Vons, *Game of Thrones*, and Sleater-Kinney, just to name a few—make the book feel uniquely regional and modern, and yet also echo the many musicians and actors and transients we've come to associate with Los Angeles and San Francisco in previous decades."
—**Levi Rogers**, *Meow Meow Pow Pow*

"Ari Rosenschein's short story collection *Coasting* takes readers inside the less-than-glamorous world of studio musicians and celebrity wannabes who are perpetually an arm's length away from their big break. These are the lives of those drawn to Los Angeles with dreams as big as the Hollywood sign, but for whom things haven't worked out so well. His stories are populated with edgy hipsters who are always a bit short when rent comes due and who can't sustain a lasting relationship, people who wish they had their lives together, but clearly do not. In other words, they're a lot like us. Rosenschein limns these lives so evocatively, we're torn between feeling smug superiority in one breath, and then complete identification in the next. A master craftsman, Rosenschein holds up a mirror to our desperate wish for something better, and the sundry ways we make peace with what is."
—**Bernadette Murphy**, author of *Harley and Me: Embracing Risk on the Road to a More Authentic Life*

"Most of *Coasting*'s linked stories occur in LA, the perfect setting for characters who trade in power and image—even when they're bad at it, even to their own demise. For these aging rockers, high school goths, tech bros, and underemployed producers, fashion is more demarcation than self-expression— their music, a path to fame, not communion. Ari Rosenschein resists explaining the deficits of these mostly male characters or embellishing their depth. He is an honest and astute chronicler of the vain and solipsistic, and though a few characters stumble into moments of insight, Rosenschein lets the rest churn in their perpetual adolescence. *Coasting* will make recovering scenesters laugh, nod, and cringe in recognition, and then give thanks they grew up."

—**Kara Vernor**, author of *Because I Wanted to Write You a Pop Song*

"The characters in *Coasting* breathe life back into the bygone era of Walkmans and used record stores, of garage bands and Myspace. These musicians, rock and roll aficionados, scenesters, producers, and fame-seekers coast through Los Angeles with eyes toward the derelict, the debauched, and the beautiful. They inhabit tattoo parlors, clubs, bodegas, studios, and grungy bathrooms while navigating divorce, desperation, dating, loneliness, and rediscovery. Rosenschein's collection is an artifact of Los Angeles—its darker corners, its bright lights, its many mysteries. With heart and grit, *Coasting* refuses to forget the past while yielding to an inescapable, transient future."

—**Nathan Elias**, author of *Coil Quake Rift and The Reincarnations*

PROCESSION

Between pockets of fresh air, through fans and fanatics, up perilous hills and pockmarked, piss-strewn avenues, down boulevards of saints and sunsets, where colts collect like cannon fodder, without limitation, throughout the universe, exclusively and in perpetuity, free and clear of any and all claims, liens and encumbrances, rights, titles and interests of any kind whatsoever, whether now known or unknown—they descend, undeterred.

HOUSE OF CINDER

I'm stewing in afternoon traffic on the 101 South, halfway between Van Nuys and Hollywood. My destination is Culture Shock Vintage Instruments on La Cienega where I'm hoping to sell my backup guitar, a Les Paul copy with an abstract painting's worth of belt buckle scratches and a tuning peg that won't stay put. Rent is due. Again. Didn't I just pay that?

I won't lie. July's been rough, and June wasn't that great either. Almost all my guitar students are on vacation except Elon, a good-natured but hyperactive nine-year-old more interested in his pet Gila monster than practicing scales. It's basically babysitting—which is fine—but I only make thirty-five dollars for the one hour, and the family lives way the hell out in the Palisades. Still, even factoring in gas, the gig helps.

We're in the middle of a string of scorchers in the highest of nineties. Brutal. Vacationing families expect this kind of heat, demand it; natives, on the other hand, consider Southern California summers penance for the region's perpetual absence of winter. As a new transplant, I feel like I haven't earned the right to complain about the climate yet. It's only been a year since I relocated from Cleveland, so I'm still untangling one Bizarro World aspect of Southern California culture or another. Like, why do people say *the* 101 as if the freeway needs a title?

It's a road, not the Count of Monte Cristo.

Today's soundtrack is the same as always: a worn cassette of AC/DC's *High Voltage* on repeat. The tape came stuck in the stereo of my '97 Ford Fiesta, which I bought off some guy named Winston in Encino. Winston didn't look like much of a rocker, but as I learned playing covers in bars back home in Ohio, AC/DC possesses a rare appeal that bridges most social divides.

"The tape won't come out, but you'll get used to it," Winston assured me. "I don't have the case anymore. Sorry."

Never bothered fixing the stereo. The tuner works fine, so if I get bored, I just flip over to KROQ for a few songs. But I always come back to *High Voltage*. Now, after countless listens, the album has become an old friend, theme music, sonic wallpaper: whatever I need it to be on a given day.

By the time I reach West Hollywood I've cycled through the AC/DC tape twice. Par for the course for a crosstown LA drive. Small miracle: I find street parking. Squinting, I walk the three exposed city blocks to Culture Shock, its red lettering and guitar-with-lightning-bolt signage glittering like an oasis in the sea of mini-malls. My belly gurgles from nerves and the Odwalla shake I had for breakfast. Selling gear is pure fucking humiliation. At least the store has air conditioning.

I push open the glass door and immediately see Kevin, the manager, with his ridiculous '70s shag and tight cowboy shirt, eyes glued to a Dell computer screen. Once upon a time, Kevin was the bassist in the Boneyard Barebacks, an early-'80s LA cowpunk band, who, according to Kevin, played Madame Wong's, Cathay de Grande, and all the other legendary punk clubs on the circuit. These details are tricky to verify, even with Google, and I haven't spent much time digging around for proof of the guy's pedigree.

He just bugs me.

There isn't much boneyard barebacking going on anymore. Kevin's music days are behind him. Basically, he manages Culture Shock and holds court, sharing unsolicited views on his favorite topic: the unremitting brutality of the music business he knows so intimately. Mostly, he loves an audience. Kevin's band veteran shtick gets old, but if I pretend to listen he might give me a couple more bucks for my beat-up guitar.

Of course, he makes me stand around for a few uncomfortable minutes before acknowledging my presence. Finally, Kevin leans over the glass counter where he keeps the rare fuzz pedals and begins today's seminar.

"Sean, you get about three years when you first move here for record labels to notice your band," he explains. "After that, you've passed your expiration date and you're shit out of luck."

"That's pretty much true," I reply, furrowing my brow and nodding like a good pupil. "Good thing my band Cinder's starting to get a little buzz. We've even had some label interest." This last bit is a lie and Kevin knows it.

"Well, stick around long enough and you *might* get some grudging respect from A&R people. That's how it was for the Boneyard Barebacks. They all knew us from hanging around the scene. Never helped us get on a major. It's a fact, Jack. No label will sign you if you're too old."

Blah blah blah. Kevin gave me this same spiel a year ago when I stopped by Culture Shock for the first time. That summer day—indistinguishable from this one, really—I was dropping off handbills for a Cinder gig at the Viper Room. Kevin looked at the flyer, snickered to his coworker, and then asked me if my band would "set the club on fire."

Ha ha. I told him I got it.

So, yeah, Kevin's a bummer. He smells how much I want a record deal and takes pleasure in reminding me of the odds because he's over the hill.

I force a laugh. Can't afford to be oversensitive. You have to show you've got a sense of humor, that you can take some ribbing. It's part of the negotiation process. "So, let's get this straight," I say, ready to parrot Kevin's advice so he'll take pity on me. "I have to hustle and make sure Cinder gets its shit together. Before we're old news."

But the lecture is over. I guess Kevin decides I've been sufficiently humiliated and he's ready to get down to business. He stands up and runs a finger through that layered Bee Gees hair. It's hard to picture the relic in front of me hanging out at the Hong Kong Café in 1980, sharing bills with X or whoever.

"Rent time again?" he says. "Let's see that piece you're selling."

"Oh yeah, this. I figure I only need one guitar right now." I surrender the instrument to him and pretend to check out a worn-looking Vox AC30 on the floor. "How much is this going for?" I ask.

Kevin doesn't answer. My interest in the amp doesn't fool either of us. He holds my guitar to his ear, strums a few chords, thumbs through a blue book, checks eBay. I can't see the screen, but I know that's what he's doing.

"$120 cash. $150 store credit."

Fucking Kevin.

When I first moved to town, I enjoyed wandering Culture Shock's rows of musty-smelling amps. Between those haphazard stacks of Fenders and Silvertones, I felt like a small stitch in the grand tapestry of LA's music history. Today, I can't wait to get out of this place. Feels like a glorified pawnshop.

Kevin knows I'm going to settle for cash. On my way out, I mutter something about coming back soon to check out the Vox.

He laughs. "See you at the end of next month, rocker."

What a prick.

Back in the car, I replay Kevin's asshole advice. I get it. I won't always be the new kid in town. I'm twenty-seven. The clock is ticking. What if Cinder isn't as good as I think? Sometimes I need a mental reset to remember why I moved here in the first place. I rewind *High Voltage* to the beginning of side one and let it play. "It's a Long Way to the Top (If You Wanna Rock 'n' Roll)" blasts out of the Ford's tinny speakers, bagpipes blaring.

For years, I daydreamed about relocating to the West Coast. I was so done with the Midwest. And not just the winters either. I just peaked there, know what I mean? I was so sick of people apologizing for having a little fucking ambition. It was impossible to get a decent band together. Everyone acted like it was a crime to try and make money playing music. Ohio was toxic, man.

Coming from a repressed shithole like Cleveland, Los Angeles was heaven. At first. Forget that self-effacing bullshit. People were big, loud, flashy—themselves with an exclamation point. I'd left things loose with my girlfriend back home, but within a week or so of bar hopping in Silver Lake I knew I had to break it off. I needed the freedom to pursue my rock dream without feeling guilty all the time. She was bummed and said I was turning into a total dick. Back in Ohio, I was pretending to be a normal dude. Here, in LA, I was the real me.

Things started happening. Within two months of arriving in town, I'd found some roommates on Craigslist, got a job in North Hollywood showing kids how to play Rage Against the Machine riffs, and formed the band. Everything felt like it was meant to be.

We went through a few names before settling on Cinder. It wasn't my first choice, but I didn't totally despise it either. (I suggested Sidewalk Fury, but the guys thought it sounded like an '80s video game.) Guess you could describe Cinder as arena-punk, like AFI meets Kings of Leon. At least that's what our bassist's girlfriend Jocelyn says when people ask. Maybe she's just humoring us. Whatever. She's more into indie stuff, anyway.

Once we had our name, Cinder concocted its master plan. Get gigs. Get a record deal. Get on the road. From there, everything would work itself out. We were each hot shit in our respective hometowns, but here in LA, we had to start from scratch. The stakes were higher.

Sometimes, when I'm lying awake because it's too hot or I'm too wound up, I think about the millions of people here trying to make it. It's such a cliché, but all of us are selling something: our words, our looks, our talent. Thinking about the competition is a surefire way to scare myself to sleep.

Lately, our drummer Mikey keeps landing acting gigs—commercials mostly—so he can't rehearse that much. He's a good-looking guy who moved out from Jersey to act. Drumming is his hobby. I get it. We all gotta do what we gotta do. Still, it's becoming a serious burden coming up with money to keep our lockout on top of my rent. Especially when we're barely practicing anymore.

I see my exit and cut across three lanes of traffic. AC/DC's "Live Wire" is playing. Mötley Crüe has a song with the same title, but I like AC/DC's better. Fuck Kevin and his attitude. He's just bitter. I'm glad I'm not that jaded. Remember how in *Charlie and the Chocolate Factory* (the book or Gene Wilder movie version, not the shitty Johnny Depp remake) everyone was looking for a golden ticket? I like to hang onto the idea that a break could be anywhere. You just have to keep your eyes open.

It's so hot. All I want to do is get back to the apartment, jerk off, rest for half an hour, then hit the rehearsal room to work on some new song ideas. Mikey said he might even come down for a bit. That would be nice.

My roommate greets me. Tony works in a warehouse, boxing porn at Vivid in North Hollywood. He has a mega-weird schedule, like a truck driver or something: on for ten days and then off for three. Whatever, I guess it works for him.

"Sean, I have to talk to you," Tony says, between slugs of Trader Joe's soy milk straight from the box. (Tony's girlfriend, Sheila, works at TJ's and gets the employee discount. He drinks gallons of the stuff.)

"This sucks, but we have someone else who wants to move in next month." Tony starts to talk faster. "It's a friend of Sheila's. I know it's been hard for you to come up with rent, and she's got a pretty steady job, so you know."

This is a major blow. It takes a moment to process the severity of Tony's statement. Sure, he's watched me barely hustle up my share most months, but I thought Tony and I were on the same page. I told the guy I was a musician the day I answered his ad. Funds get a little tight sometimes.

I wait a beat and try to come up with a new angle. "Dude, it's just the summer," I finally plead. "Lessons always slow down this time of year. Look, I just sold my backup guitar. I can make rent."

"I told you, it sucks." He takes another swig from his soy milk and throws the empty box in the garbage can. "I gotta rest up. Sheila and I are going to see *Pee Wee's Big Adventure* at Hollywood Forever Cemetery later." Tony turns around and walks toward his bedroom.

Fucking Tony. He gets the place and the girlfriend. Sheila is probably in there right now waiting for him in nothing but her green Trader Joe's shirt and panties. She walks around the apartment like that all the time when she stays over. Thank god for the promo DVDs that Tony floats me from Vivid. My sex life has been pretty much nonexistent lately. I've been too stressed about money and the band to get into a hookup headspace.

"Don't I get like two weeks' notice or something?" I yell at Tony's back.

He turns around and sighs. "Sean, this isn't a job. It's not like there's a contract. We met you through a Craigslist ad." He waits a second. "You can stay on the couch for a few days while you look for a room."

Thanks.

I flop face down on my futon and scheme. Out of the corner of my eye, I see the Fender practice amp that came with me from Ohio. Kevin might give me something for that thing. Stacked up next to the amp is a pile of DVDs: mostly raunchy titles, with concert movies by Green Day and Muse thrown in. Maybe I can sell a few of them at Amoeba. I can't think in here, and I don't even feel like jerking off anymore. Impending homelessness kills the mood.

The only choice is to head to the rehearsal space—the House of Cinder as we like to call it. I hop in the Fiesta, and there are Bon Scott, Angus Young, and the rest of AC/DC in their usual positions. I turn the stereo off. Not right now. I need quiet.

My mind races through frantic financial formulas. Somehow, I make it to our lockout. It's dark and cool in here. When I feel this bad, all I want to do is bang on Mikey's kit. Drums aren't my main instrument so I'm pretty terrible, but it's cathartic. I sit on the throne and pound out caveman versions of "Enter Sandman," "Smells Like Teen Spirit," some Offspring and Rancid songs. I miss the snare a bunch and beat up my knuckles. Shit, it feels good to play.

You're not supposed to do this, but I know for a fact there are guys who actually live in their rehearsal studios. One time I was here late and got drunk with this dude Scott who has a bunk built in his room and everything.

No one seems to mess with him. If I had to, I guess I could do that for a while. Truth is, I'd have just as much room as at Tony's apartment and I'm already paying for this place.

Then I remember the half-eaten block of Valentine's chocolate I noticed on top of Scott's sleeping bag. I hate thinking of him in there, nibbling on cheap, deteriorating candy. Who gave it to him in the first place? Whatever, even if it came to that, staying here would be a temporary solution. A few months at the most while I figure things out.

I pull my guitar out of its gig bag and pluck at the opening riff of the Chili Peppers "Under the Bridge." It's the lamest, most self-pitying thing I can think of. My phone buzzes. I see Mikey's number. I answer. He can't rehearse tonight. An audition for an AT&T ad tomorrow.

Maybe playing a song from *High Voltage* will cheer me up, but I don't actually know any of them on guitar. Instead, I strum the chorus of "You Shook Me All Night Long." It sounds good unplugged, more melancholy. Almost like a different song.

MEET CUTE

Matt had been sitting in front of Intelligentsia Coffee in Silver Lake for two hours—or was it more like three? He'd finished a crossword puzzle and a pack of Camels and seen a barista shift turn over. 11:30 a.m. on a Tuesday at Sunset Junction. Aggressively bright out—typical for October, really—but pleasant under the awning. Matt's mouth tasted of coffee and nicotine. He wriggled in his seat, conscious of a fierce need to urinate yet unwilling to give up his choice table.

Since he and Kelly split up, Matt spent mornings at Intelligentsia with religious consistency. He liked the way the cafe sheltered the displaced, independently wealthy, and jobless. Matt was somewhere in the middle. He eked out a living scoping eBay for movie memorabilia, toggling between a few auctions at a time, then swooping in at the last minute to nab the prize. (Last week, he scored a vintage *Blade Runner* poster, turned it around, and tripled his money.) Mostly, though, he drank expensive coffees and checked out girls.

Today, there were many: Los Feliz moms, mats strapped to their backs, flushed with post-Yoga color; pale punkettes with sleeves of bright, trust fund tattoos; and even the occasional UCLA co-ed, as conspicuous at this Eastside haunt as Matt's dinged-up Honda was in Westwood.

He remembered one of his last arguments with Kelly. She was packing up her share of the kitchen supplies. By that point, their battles were more icy than impassioned.

"I've never met someone so hung up on their image," she told him, looking up from boxing her Hello Kitty toaster. "You wear that *Aliens* T-shirt and those same skinny jeans every day." Kelly tilted her head to the side. She always did that before driving a point home. "You're thirty-six," she said. "Deal."

Matt parried. "Oh, but you deciding to divorce me so you can fuck girls again isn't indicative of a midlife crisis?" Of course, Kelly had dated girls in college, before he knew her, but Matt always figured that was early-twenties stuff. Experimenting.

Of course, she was right. Matt knew he was stuck in a holding pattern. He'd taken his eye off the ball, spending entire days lost in online film forums, kicking around the same unfinished screenplay for years.

As he floundered, Kelly grew more and more into herself. First, it was the assistant-to-the-director job at the Los Angeles Boys & Girls Club, then the meditation seminars. Eventually, she met Bonnie at the Self-Realization Fellowship. And that was that.

Matt sniffed his fingers—sweet like processed tobacco—and lit a cigarette. Reflecting on a five-year marriage required another smoke.

They'd first met at the Saturday night AA meeting at Café Tropical. Later that evening, he dug around her Myspace page. In her profile pic, Kelly wore a *Bride of Chucky* Halloween costume. Sex, movie kitsch, and menace in the same package; she was his ideal.

At first, their AA connection was a good thing. Matt found that maintaining his sobriety was easier with a non-drinking partner. Later, though, Kelly started using twelve-step talk to cut him down. She had a latent talent for this, wielding Big Book phrases like "emotional immaturity" and "constitutionally incapable of being honest" to remind Matt of the years he drank away after college, working at Vidiots.

Matt closed one eBay tab on his MacBook, intermittently checking out two girls at the adjacent table. One had a bleached blonde cut, long on top but shaved underneath. She wore a striped romper and high-top sneakers, a look that took him back to high school in the '90s, before she was born. Everything old was new again, he thought. The other girl wore her dark hair in an angled bob and had on high-waisted shorts with an off-the-shoulder T-shirt. Both had cute little bodies, he noted, and were at least fifteen years his junior. Matt looked away, feeling sleazy.

The dark-haired one got up and went to the bathroom. Matt saw a line of women standing with arms crossed near the community bulletin board. A chubby dude in an OBEY shirt grabbed a sticker-covered spatula attached to a key and entered the men's room. No wait. Yet another travail girls face daily, he thought.

Next to him, the blonde picked up a fat paperback and placed a unicorn bookmark on the table.

"What are you reading?" Matt asked.

"It's the second *Game of Thrones*," she replied, looking at the back cover.

Matt leaned in and took off his sunglasses. "That guy's a total misogynist. You know that, right?"

She didn't reply, just opened the book and started reading.

Matt returned to his phone and considered his options. "Everyone says that guy invented the whole off-the-page magic thing," he said. "I think people mostly buy his books for the sex and slaughter."

"I'm kind of into it," she said without looking up.

"Sorry," Matt said. "Martin just pisses me off."

No answer. She picked up her coffee. He seized the moment.

"It's great to see someone reading. I've been hanging here all day and nobody's even cracked a book. People are just sitting, not doing a goddamn thing." He laughed at his Holden Caulfield rant.

The dark-haired friend returned, and the girls began talking about how picked over Melrose Trading Post had become lately.

Since breaking up with Kelly and becoming a single adult in Los Angeles, Matt discovered he hated dating and its formalities: meeting times, dinner, forced conversation. The fuzzy, horny mess of a bar pickup was less complicated. Last weekend was typical.

A girl at The Short Stop in Echo Park told Matt he looked like an indie Matthew McConaughey. He could only make out every other word she was saying, but he picked up that she liked Wes Anderson movies. All of a sudden, it was 2 a.m. Then there was that desperate push for the door, the closing of the deal.

Really, though, Matt was lonely. At night in his cramped apartment, he pictured Kelly and Bonnie snuggled up on the couch in Bonnie's Eagle Rock home, a classic bungalow filled with CB2 furniture and hand-poured candles with names like Deersong and Cotton Candy Daydream.

Round two. "I used to hit the Fairfax flea market," Matt said. "But now I only do the Rose Bowl. It's more old-school." He was trying for an air of confidence to soften his intrusion, establish a conversational foothold.

The brunette sighed but went with it. "Yeah, Rose Bowl is

good for, like, old stuff. I find the best '80s band T-shirts on Melrose, though." She laughed. She wasn't as pretty as her friend, but possibly smarter, and Matt liked her unkempt eyebrows. She had small green eyes and a Grecian nose. She was actually very cute.

"What kind of movies are you guys into?" Matt asked, attempting to bring the blonde back into the conversation. "I'm going to see *The Hateful Eight* at the Vista at 12:45." They both looked confused. "Quentin Tarantino wrote it. It's got Samuel Jackson, Jennifer Jason Leigh. A bunch of other actors."

"Who?" the brunette asked, genuinely interested.

The blonde looked over at Matt. Was she irritated that he was making inroads with her friend?

Then, a surprise. "I'll go," said the blonde before adding, "I mean, I don't have any classes today."

Following her lead, the brunette, too, became amenable. "Yeah, sounds good."

Matt went back to his laptop for a second. Didn't want to betray his shock at the unexpected success of the maneuver. "Cool," he said. And meant it. "I'm Matt."

The brunette rose from her seat. "I'm Tracy," she said.

The blonde put down her fantasy novel, stood up, and stretched. "It's 12:30. We should get to the theater. Shannon, by the way."

The girls invited him to smoke some pot before the movie. He politely declined without mentioning he'd been clean and sober for five years. Matt knew he was particularly vulnerable to marijuana. Being around that drug was—as his sponsor was fond of saying—like hanging out in a bad neighborhood.

As the lights dimmed in the vintage Art Deco theater, Matt thought about how decadent it felt to be at a midday movie.

Usually at this hour, he was still at Intelligentsia, pretending to work.

The film was typical Tarantino: verbose and absurdly over-violent. At one point, fatigued by the movie's sensory barrage, Matt started to invent scenarios that could end with Tracy and Shannon in his bed. He peeked at Tracy, who had one leg pulled onto her seat. She caught him looking and smiled, then returned to the bounty hunter saga. Kelly would never believe he could get two girls he didn't even know to go to a Tarantino movie with him.

Walking into the bright light of Sunset, with the Morricone score still in his head, Matt's hopes disintegrated. It was almost 4 p.m. Was it really that late? God, Tarantino's movies were long. Getting a girl to go home with him at last call one thing. With the working world whizzing by, seduction seemed impossible.

He had to act fast. "What are you up to now? I live off of Heliotrope, near the Ukrainian Cultural Center. There's a cool meditation hall there." Why did he say that? He hated that place. Kelly used to go there all the time.

"I have to study," Shannon said firmly, crossing her arms in front of her. "Or get baked and go to sleep, then study. I'm burnt. I'm going home." She raised an eyebrow at her friend.

Tracy looked at her and then at Matt. At that precise moment, Matt knew—if he played his cards right—he could fuck Tracy today.

"I don't have anything going on. I'll check out that meditation place," she said.

"Whatever," said Shannon, pulling keys out of her bag. "See you back at the place."

Matt gave Tracy directions to his apartment. Somehow,

they both found spots nearby. He walked her around the neighborhood, planning to stop at Scoops, an artisanal ice cream shop near where the Bicycle Cafe used to be. (Where *did* that place go?)

As they strolled, Matt learned that Tracy grew up in Utah and only moved to LA a year and a half ago to start school at Occidental. She and Shannon met as freshmen in a comp and rhetoric course and stayed friends.

"We clicked really easily," Tracy said. She looked at the ground as she talked. Matt caught a hint of sadness around her eyes he hadn't noticed earlier. "Shannon can be bossy, but she's really smart. She's from Anaheim, so she knows LA really well."

He disputed that last fact but nodded. Matt realized he enjoyed showing off his Eastside domain, being the guy who knew all the cool spots. He nodded at a group of younger guys from AA as they walked into the neighborhood pizza place.

"You're gonna love Scoops," Matt said, keeping his tour guide routine going. "They have the craziest flavors.

Lemongrass ice cream, stuff like that." He asked the guy behind the counter for a few tasters of the Vanilla Bean Himalayan Sea Salt and had just taken them in both hands when he heard a thud.

Matt spun on his heel and saw Tracy on the floor, convulsing wildly. Hands twisted inward on themselves at severe angles, tongue lolled outside the mouth. Matt froze and tried to remember what he was supposed to do in a situation like this.

A crusty street punk was spare-changing in front of Scoops. He peeked around the door from the ground. "Dude, your girlfriend is having a grand mal seizure," he slurred.

Matt put both sample spoons on the counter (more gently

than he felt the situation warranted) and dropped down. He reached and held the back of Tracy's head, stopping it from banging against the ground.

"Put your hand in her mouth so she doesn't bite her tongue," the crusty yelled from outside. "My ex used to have these all the time."

Matt waited for an opening. Finding none, he used his forefinger and thumb to winch open Tracy's mouth. Once inside, Matt held her slippery tongue in a pincer-like claw, teeth chattering against his knuckles. He had no idea if this was the correct seizure-response form, but it felt like a confident, impressive action: the right thing to do.

Matt looked to the door for approval, but the crusty was no longer watching. Tracy's pupils were out of view, eyes alabaster, but her weight felt good in his arms, grounding him. Her shirt rode up her belly as she convulsed in his lap. He pulled it down. As Tracy writhed, Matt was aware of his cock stirring slightly in his jeans.

He remembered Kelly telling him how gross it was that he was turned on after watching *Audition*, a Japanese cult horror flick. "It's not supposed to be sexy," she said as she sipped her Thai Iced Tea, "when she's hacking up that guy. It's disturbing."

He couldn't explain that it wasn't a voluntary reaction, the way the violence and teasing and foreignness of the flick congealed into an erotic brew. "I'm not saying the killing part made me horny. It was just the whole weird, kinky vibe of the movie," he sputtered. Kelly made a fake stabbing motion with her fork and twirled a few Rad Na noodles off Matt's plate.

Tracy came to and brought him back into the moment, into Scoops, into the reality of cradling the neck of a young lady from Utah he barely knew. She was disoriented, weak and blinking, cheeks wet from involuntary tears.

"Hey there," Matt said, sounding more protective than he expected. "I was just grabbing our order and you went down."

"This is so embarrassing. They hardly ever happen anymore. I'm sorry." Tracy sat up, and Matt could see a little bit of her underwear where the corners of her thighs met her pubis. He looked away. The moment the episode began, she'd gone from a prize to his responsibility.

Matt put his hand on Tracy's shoulder and helped her up. "It's no problem. Let's just relax for a sec. We can sit down over here." He walked her over to a circular two-top by the wall. The counter guy brought over their cones, which, miraculously, hadn't melted. Matt thanked him with a nod and turned back to Tracy. She sat, hands in her lap, eyes downcast, much younger than he'd allowed himself to notice before.

"I used to get them more in Provo. You won't believe this. Shannon doesn't even know I'm epileptic. That's how rare it is that I seize." Tracy seemed relieved to speak freely. Matt listened and ate his red bean ice cream, quickly making it down to the cone. This place was really good.

He sat with her for a while, listening mostly, absorbed in the story of Tracy from Utah who moved to LA who liked Passion Pit and The National who had won a hefty scholarship to attend Occidental who had one brother back home older than her who had a bit of a failure to launch thing going on and sold pot out of his bedroom which was actually kind of cool because he hooked her up with weed but she really should stop smoking so much especially on epilepsy medication look what happened today good thing Matt was here since it could have been really bad.

Matt remembered how much he'd wanted to bring her back to his apartment and winced at the thought of a seizure behind closed doors. Somehow, it was more acceptable in public. At least bystanders could applaud his valiant effort.

After sitting with Tracy from Utah for nearly an hour, then reluctantly letting her drive home, Matt sprawled out on his IKEA futon and returned to watching *Band of Brothers* on DVD. Still basking in the heroic afterglow, he couldn't wait to slip into the monochrome trenches and noisy mess halls of the HBO series. Matt needed to be around men. Even fictional ones. Their trench banter and collective sexual frustration would close the day out nicely.

Matt's phone buzzed on the floor. He remembered asking Tracy to text when she got home. It felt like the stand-up thing to say.

Hey, thanks for everything. Sorry for the weird afternoon. Text me sometime if you want. -T

Matt wondered if Tracy told her roommate (what was her name again?) about their afternoon and decided probably not. He wondered if Tracy was off limits now and considered deleting her number. Fuck it. He texted back.

No worries. Glad you made it home.

Then, in a separate bubble.

Crazy movie, right?

LANDMARK

Liliya and Rick greeted Saul from behind the screen door of their Los Feliz apartment. Saul was wearing his uniform of tight black jeans, Converse, and a denim jacket covered with patches and pins—first wave punk and obscure '90s Olympia bands mostly. In spite of the pulverizing late summer heat and his Pabst gut, he'd walked all the way from his apartment near Gower Gulch.

Liliya (still committed to her punk thing well into her late thirties) leaned in and kissed him on the cheek. Beneath a thick wall of MAC foundation lay the distrustful countenance of a Russian grandmother. Her husband Rick was a good-looking guy with a formidable pompadour; he too was hanging onto a fading look for dear life.

"Come in, honey," said Liliya. "Everybody else is here already."

Saul wiped his forehead; it was waxy with sweat and hair product. Parties like this were not his scene. He'd met the hosts at Flyover Records, the vinyl-only store at Sunset Junction where he worked Tuesday through Saturday. Saul had helped Rick find a rare Cramps LP. Turned out they had some friends in common, so when Liliya invited him to a "thing we're doing at the house," Saul wasn't surprised, just anxious. Despite the subtle distinction between having and *doing* a thing, it sounded like a typical Eastside get-together: an unbearable proposition. Still, with no girlfriend and the day off work, Saul didn't refuse. Forced socializing was the only kind that got him out of the house lately.

He entered the living room wearing a half smile he thought made his doughy face look more like Darby Crash. (When anyone asked, Saul claimed he moved to Los Angeles from Eugene, Oregon, solely based on his obsession with LA punk rock bands like the Germs and the Screamers.) There were three other Flyover regulars already at the party. Saul relaxed at the sight of familiar faces and greeted each with what he felt was the appropriate amount of conviviality: side hug for Suzie, a sturdy blonde who worked at Squaresville on Vermont; full embrace for Rene, who styled hair for reality TV and resembled Joan Jett; finally, a firm handshake for Rene's boyfriend Al, a tall guy with a goatee who did something involving real estate. Suzie offered him a spot on the vintage couch.

Rick dashed into the kitchen and returned with beer and sodas. Saul sucked in his stomach and attempted to brood like John Doe from X while the other three gabbed glibly about some lame band called Colorhaze who just played Spaceland, an *Entourage* cast member sighting at Home Depot, and the city's current oppressive heatwave. In the corner, a chunky vintage iPod served up songs from a Link Wray playlist. Pleasant enough, but why wouldn't the hosts stop pacing?

Without warning, it was showtime. Standing in the center of the room, Liliya pulled out a colorful pamphlet with a beaming gray-haired couple on the cover. "So, here's the deal," she said, then explained that she and Rick just completed the Landmark Forum and had life-changing insights to share.

Liliya's introductory spiel came at a pace bordering on manic.

Within minutes, Saul felt the room get at least ten degrees hotter. He pulled his jacket off and wiped his palms on his thighs.

Saul knew all about Landmark. The group was kind of an updated version of EST, the '70s celebrity cult of choice. Liliya and Rick, the friendly rockabilly scenesters, had been body snatched; in their place stood two glassy-eyed dogma dispensers.

Time crawled as Liliya droned on in labyrinthine Forum-speak. "There's what you know, what you don't know, and then there's what you don't know you don't know," she said obscurely.

Rick punctuated every other line with a jovial "absolutely" or "exactly" or "I thought it was crazy too," an amiable Flavor Flav to his wife's Chuck D. Saul wriggled in his seat, crossing and uncrossing his legs. He tried to catch the eye of another attendee for some confirmation of the utter bizarreness they were witnessing. All three had plastic smiles.

Seemingly oblivious to the mood of her audience, Liliya advanced aggressively through the indoctrination script. "Sign up for a seminar," she told them. "Just a weekend. How will you know unless you try?"

Cults were such an LA thing. Saul remembered this guy he knew who fancied himself a punk rock spiritual guru or some shit. His devotees seriously thought they were members of an edgy, anti-authority movement. Sometimes, the guru guy came by the record store and tried to act down by talking about obscure hardcore seven-inches. Off the meditation pillow, the dude bragged about gambling wins in Las Vegas, ate McDonalds, and was constantly touting the self-help books he'd written. Saul found him exhausting.

The whole deal was mostly hippy shit, reheated Eastern

principles, but Saul attended a New Year's Eve "intention-setting" ritual anyway. He was curious. Midway through the interminable ceremony, the congregants passed around a collection plate into which he placed a ten-dollar bill before taking seven back as change. Afterward, an irate member confronted Saul in the lobby and accused him of stealing from the group. So much for positive intentions.

Back in the living room, Rick was going on about how honest he felt since the Forum, how satisfying his work was since the Forum, how much better he and Liliya understood each other since the Forum. Saul needed a breather. He announced (with as much innocent enthusiasm as he could muster) that he had to take a serious piss.

Without taking an eye off her captive audience, Liliya pointed a hot pink nail in the direction of the kitchen. "OK, sweetie. It's right next to the laundry room."

The light blue bathroom contained a velvet Elvis poster and nautical-themed shower curtain—among other tchotchkes. Saul closed his eyes and slowed his breathing. He examined himself in the mirror: spiky hair, hand-poked knuckle tattoos, perfectly faded Crass T-shirt. Cursing his paunch, but otherwise bolstered by the reflection, he flushed the toilet and ran the faucet for added believability. Right before opening the door, he glared at the mirror like a young Henry Rollins. My war, he thought.

Rene was waiting in the kitchen. Saul figured she also needed a break from the barrage of bullshit. "What is this, fucking Amway?" Saul whispered, probably too loudly. He didn't care anymore. He felt duped by this whole thing and wanted Liliya and Rick to hear him complain.

Rene mouthed an exaggerated "I know" and slipped into the

bathroom.

Back on the couch, Liliya lasered in on Saul. "I know you're not a joiner," she explained, now attempting to appeal to his iconoclastic spirit, "but this isn't about being a member of a group. It's about you. This is a gift to yourself." Liliya slapped him on the knee for emphasis. He felt his Rollins resolve slipping away. "Think of what you could do for the Eastside music scene. You always talk about starting a label. What's really stopping you?"

She was right. Most of his co-workers at Flyover had launched bedroom imprints while he drank and pretended not to care about success. Outwardly, he judged their DIY ventures as "a bunch of LA bullshit," but he envied their stupid, focused passion. Deep down he feared that starting a label—doing anything, really—was too much of a commitment, the first step on the slippery slope to conformity.

There was a creepy guy named Zack who'd been trying to get Saul to invest in his label idea. No one knew much about him. He came by the record store a lot, talking a big game, about how he knew indie distributors like ADA and Revolver. He went out with this older goth girl named Reegan who Saul knew from Squaresville. The Eastside was pretty provincial.

Wielding a sign-up clipboard, Rick brought up the rear. "People who do the weekend end up with these incredible realizations about themselves." Take the flyer, Saul thought. Do the fucking weekend. Anything to get these two to stop. Just do it. What can it hurt?

But then he heard the voice of Rollins.

Get
the fuck
out of here.

"You guys," he said. "I can't right now. It's not a good time. I can tell this Forum thing has been great for you both, but I have a lot going on. I hope you get it."

Saul knew he sounded more like a nebbish than a nonconformist. Still, it seemed to work. Disappointed but acquiescent, Liliya moved on to the remaining guests. Rene and Al stood their ground, but Suzie was not so lucky. The hosts cornered her; the promise of broadened economic horizons proved too tempting.

Sensing an opening, the three of them gathered their things and bid hasty goodbyes while Liliya prepped a shell-shocked Suzie for an upcoming Landmark weekend. They got her, Saul thought.

Outside, Rene and Al walked arm in arm through the thick August heat. Saul trailed behind, hands shoved in jean jacket pockets, adrenaline still pumping from the encounter. They invited him for tacos near Vermont which sounded pretty good. The escapees laughed nervously as they stood outside the silver-plated truck.

"What the fuck was that?" Saul asked, picking a piece of cilantro from between his teeth.

Rene rolled her eyes. "I've been to that kind of thing before. When I was a kid, my mom was all mixed up in some cult shit. They cleaned her out." She looked down at the street, black shag falling forward, covering her face.

Saul wished he could leave it alone, forget the whole afternoon, discuss the Dodgers, the weather, anything. But he felt it starting, the twin sparks of mutual disapproval and righteous indignation which fueled the best shit-talking sessions.

"Did you see their eyes?" Saul asked, milking the disbelief out of every syllable. "There is nothing more LA than that shit.

A self-help cult, what a cliché."

Al played devil's advocate. "I don't know? They looked pretty happy."

Saul added some hot sauce to his second taco; this place was a little bland. "Seekers. City is made of them," he said between bites. "They come to LA vulnerable and ambitious. What do you expect?"

The sun was starting to come down, clouds turning pink in the hazy sky. It had been a long afternoon. Rene jumped to Rick's defense. "What about you, Saul? Isn't record collecting kind of a cult? You and your buddies at the store get pretty pious about your opinions."

"But we're not proselytizing."

"OK, you're elitists, not cultists," Rene replied with unconcealed bile. She looked to Al and motioned that it was time to go. They said their goodbyes and walked in the opposite direction. Saul decided to float around Los Feliz for a bit. Rene was right, he thought. He'd been an asshole.

The evening Santa Ana winds brought new energy to his step as he walked up Sunset. He took a left on L. Ron Hubbard Way and approached one of the ominous Scientology buildings. Los Angeles held many mysteries for Saul when he first arrived from Eugene, none as baffling as the far-reaching tentacles of Scientology, whose tacky trappings coated the city.

He peered into a window display and read a testimonial written by Chick Corea. The jazz fusion legend's gobbledygook sounded just like Liliya and Rick. Saul observed a cluster of besuited young people gathered around a doorway smoking cigarettes: Scientology's worker bees. He laughed. Had to be careful in this city; you could get snatched up anywhere.

Hollywood night fell. He passed Normandie and kept going.

Not ready to head home yet, he decided to overshoot his apartment. Keep this pace and he might even make it to Amoeba before they closed to poke through the new arrivals. Saul imagined himself the last holdout in a city of seekers, Rollins walking beside him, whispering in his ear.

ANY DAY NOW

Ava tidied the rehearsal room and waited for Jocelyn. She bopped around, butterflies in her stomach, the Pixies in her earbuds. It must be a Virgo thing, she thought—this need to have everything in order: cables coiled and resting on amps, guitar cases stacked neatly by the door, jade incense burning. The deep clean was Ava's little gift to both of them—to Blue Spark, the band they formed just a few months ago.

She even brought a broom from home to sweep the ancient carpet. Before today, it had been just her and Jocelyn joking around and writing songs, but tonight Blue Spark was auditioning a drummer. Or maybe it was the other way around. Her name was Charlie and she was a Silver Lake icon. So, everything had to look great.

Unlike Ava, Jocelyn didn't care much about tidiness or appearances at all. She didn't have to, Ava often thought. They weren't opposites, though, more like complementary colors. Effortlessly thin, Jocelyn had long brown Coachella hair and an ethereal singing voice. Ava's raspy howl was informed by lots of Sleater-Kinney and Frank Black; she'd been dying her blunt bob black for so long that natural hair color was a distant memory.

Things came easily for Jocelyn. Even her messy apartment on

Vermont felt more lived-in than uncared-for, a byproduct of an innate chillness. Her folks still paid her rent every month. For spending money, she designed flyers for Los Globos and worked a shift or two a week at White Trash Charms on Hillhurst. It was, as Jocelyn liked to say, all good.

Friends at UC Riverside, Ava and Jocelyn both moved to Los Feliz in a post-college decision-making frenzy. Ava had been a Museum Studies major and quickly found work as an administrative assistant at the Hammer Museum. Jocelyn, on the other hand, wasn't putting her BA to any particular use. Blue Spark was the most serious thing she had going on. Other than the band, she was coasting.

Meeting a local legend like Charlie required the perfect getup, so Ava assembled a Silver Lake-boho-musician look: jeans from Urban Outfitters, mock jewelry mixed in with a few expensive pieces, and Vans slip-ons with Iron Maiden artwork she bought at the outlets last month. The shoes were a little tribute to her and Jocelyn: nice girls who were gonna have to be tough chicks to make a dent in the music world. Whatever. It made sense in the store.

Neither member wanted people to think of Blue Spark as another girl band (not that anyone was thinking of them at all), but they also agreed on a no-guys-in-the-lineup policy. They couldn't imagine playing with dudes, especially the muso types who talked down to them. Those creeps were unbearable.

Jocelyn and Ava had been talking about Blue Spark since they were at Riverside, but once they committed to the idea, things came together quickly. The first song they wrote in their Echo Park practice space was called "Any Day Now."

No one to wait up for me

I guess I have to get used to being free

That thing I always knew I'd need
Is coming any day now

After that, they repeated the song title a whole bunch of times and left a good spot open for a solo. Ava hoped they'd add a second guitar player to handle the flourishes.

Bored with work and making decent money for the first time, Ava bought a Fender Jaguar from Culture Shock in West Hollywood. Right out of school, Jocelyn started dating this guy Peter who played bass in Cinder, a lame Sunset Strip pseudo-alternative band neither of them liked. They broke up (Jocelyn and Peter, not Cinder, sadly), but Jocelyn picked up bass from her ex. In fact—much to his annoyance—she flew past him on the instrument. Joy Division lines, some Cure, Nirvana, Silversun Pickups. Bass suited her. With that spooky voice and bulky instrument, Jocelyn reminded Ava of the bassists in Hole or Smashing Pumpkins. She had the whole aloof '90s-style thing down without even trying.

Jocelyn burst through the door and dropped her fringed purse on the floor, a pack of yellow American Spirits spilling out. "I am so pumped," she said. "Fucking Charlie from Retriever jamming with Blue Spark. I love it." She picked up her bass from where Ava had lovingly placed it against her amp and looked around at the clean studio. "It smells good in here."

Ava smiled at Jocelyn's excitement. She was excited too. Charlie had played in a string of nearly legendary indie acts they followed in college, bands like Pillow Talk, Lawn Vultures, and Retriever. The girls had been listening to Charlie's records for years and were supremely starstruck when they started seeing her out and about at Swingers and various music venues. How was she not in a band anymore? Charlie was the missing ingredient Blue Spark needed. Following a late Saturday night at Shortstop, the girls, feeling brave, concocted a plan.

Giggling like seventh graders, huddled around the iPad Jocelyn's parents bought her as a graduation gift, they composed a sassy Facebook message to Charlie and pressed send, assuming they'd never hear from her. To their surprise, Charlie wrote back the next day saying she loved the two boombox demos posted on Blue Spark's SoundCloud page and wanted to jam.

They were running through one of those songs when Charlie walked in, sticker-covered snare drum case in hand. She took off her aviator shades and scanned the room.

"Hey ladies. Where should I set up my kit?"

From somewhere high in the ceiling, Ava heard herself babbling and pointing out the freshly swept corner of the jam room. As she set up her drums, Charlie appeared so in her element. Compared to this pro, she and Jocelyn were obvious newbies.

Ava couldn't believe how tiny the drummer looked in her Levi's and high-top Converse. Also, Charlie was obviously gay. Like, Chrome Hearts rings and rainbow necklace gay. Ava realized, during all the hours she'd spent staring at Pillow Talk's album cover, she never considered the sexuality of the band members. Somehow Charlie being a lesbian just reinforced how babyish Ava felt.

After tightening her ride cymbal, Charlie placed the mirrored sunglasses back on and stretched her arms out behind her back. So feline, thought Ava.

"I loved Pillow Talk," Ava said. "I listened to your album all the time. It was the soundtrack to my senior year in high school."

Charlie laughed. "Senior year. Right. I forget you two are still youngsters. Yeah, PT's record was pretty cool. Would have been better if the producer hadn't buried the kick drum in the final mix."

Ava didn't know what to say. "I think your drumming rules on that album."

Charlie tuned her snare and tapped it a few times. "Let's play that first one from SoundCloud," she said. The song, a fast tune called "Tony Has a Tude," was about a belligerent bartender they knew from the Dresden on Vermont. Jocelyn and Ava had been hoping she'd want to start with that one. It was easy to play so they could rock out a bit.

Charlie counted them in.

And in their cramped, cheap incense-filled rehearsal space, "Tony Has a Tude" sounded better than the girls had ever imagined. Charlie must have agreed because right when they finished, she looked at them both and said, "OK, let's work on the transition into the last chorus from the bridge."

They'd written a bridge? What was that?

Was Charlie their drummer?

For Ava, the next few weeks were a blur of practices, post-rehearsal meals at Fred 62, and days at the Hammer, breezier now that she had the delicious daydream of Blue Spark's completed lineup to distract her.

Hanging out as a threesome was a whole other thing. Jocelyn and Ava were different from Charlie, and it wasn't just their ages. Their new member was a little out of the loop musically. ("Arctic Monkeys? Do they sing 'Daydream Believer'? I'm just fucking with you. But seriously, who are they?") Charlie also had a massive personality, often hijacking conversations to tell a story about a former bandmate who'd wronged her or recount tour bus shenanigans.

Charlie knew everyone in the Eastside music community

and was anxious to book Blue Spark its first gig. In fact, she became obsessed with the idea, drilling its importance every opportunity she got. "We've got to start playing live. Like yesterday. I've got the itch." Finally, at the beginning of a Sunday night rehearsal, Charlie announced she'd booked the band a show at The Echo opening for the Scarlet Letters, a surf garage act from San Diego with a big following.

"Aren't they kind of huge?" Jocelyn asked.

Ava's heart fluttered with excitement and fear. The show felt like a dare. Sure, she wanted to do gigs—that was the whole point—but she was concerned that she and Jocelyn had never performed in front of anyone. Ever. "Maybe we should wait until me and Joss catch up to you a bit, get tighter," she offered.

Charlie disagreed. "Fuck that. You two were ready the day I got your Facebook message," Charlie said. "This is like losing your live virginity. You just have to get it over with and move on."

The imminent performance changed the mood at rehearsal that night. Picturing an audience watching, they attacked their songs with a new energy. Afterward, the three members of Blue Spark went to Fred 62 and shared two orders of sweet potato fries.

"Holy shit," Ava said. "The Echo gig is only three weeks away."

Jocelyn looked down at her plate. She didn't really speak her mind yet with Charlie around, preferring to confide in Ava after the fact.

Charlie snorted. "Plenty of time to get shit tight. In Retriever, we recorded our whole first album in twelve hours."

The next three weeks were band boot camp. Charlie showed them how to craft a set for maximum impact, stacking the most rocking numbers at the front and leaving holes between songs for stage banter. She gave them invaluable tips, like not looking at their hands all the time when they played. They repeated the set until Ava's callouses felt impermeable, her already-throaty voice the most authoritative it had ever sounded.

Show day came, and Ava was a wreck. She couldn't focus at work and kept going over the set in her mind. Once she arrived home, after battling traffic on the 10 Freeway, Ava changed her outfit three times, finally settling on a white tank top and pleated skirt. She thought it was a bit riot grrrl-light, but it couldn't hurt to place Blue Spark in some kind of musical lineage people understood. Also, Ava liked the way her legs looked in the skirt.

She raced to The Echo for soundcheck. The churning in her stomach subsided a bit, or maybe it just turned into adrenaline. Ava couldn't tell. The Scarlet Letters were finishing the last song of their check. They sounded super-tight and had a huge painted backdrop hanging behind the stage. It was obvious who was headlining tonight.

Ava saw Jocelyn sitting on the floor near the side of the stage, tuning and retuning her bass.

"I am fucking freaking out," she stage-whispered to Ava.

"Me too," Ava said, though seeing Jocelyn, she felt better than she had all day.

That was when things got weird.

Five minutes later, Charlie showed up at the venue decked out in leather pants, huge biker boots, and a crazy sliced-up T-shirt that looked like something from an *SNL* sketch. Ava tried to conceal the shock she knew was creeping over her face. (She was useless at hiding her feelings.) Where was the Charlie from the past two months of rehearsal? Tonight, their drummer looked like a lost member of some '80s glam group.

It hadn't occurred to Ava that Blue Spark would ever have to discuss stage wear. For Jocelyn and her, it was an unspoken thing, part of the same easy vibe that made their musical connection and friendship work. Ava accepted that Charlie was a bit long in the tooth, but she never expected their new member to veer this far off script. She was the ex-drummer of Pillow Talk, not Poison.

Charlie made a beeline for the members of the Scarlet Letters, who had congregated at the bar for pre-show drinks. Ava watched as—aviator shades firmly in place—Charlie hugged the lead singer and the guitarist. Clearly, they were old friends of hers from the scene. Charlie stood talking and laughing loudly with them for a solid ten minutes before motioning that she had to go and grab her drums. At that point, Charlie left the club to get her gear from the car.

"She didn't even say hi to us," said Jocelyn.

Ava raised her eyebrows. "Did you see those Jim Morrison pants?"

Jocelyn sighed. "It's all good. Help me with my stuff."

The two of them hoisted their amps onstage and started plugging instruments into effects pedals.

Charlie eventually sauntered up, sunglasses in place, and dropped her drum cases in front of the riser. As she assembled her kit, she monologued to no one in particular. "It's been a minute since I played here. Last time was with Pillow Talk." She tried out the kick drum. "I killed it in that band. Too bad the singer was a douche."

With Charlie yet to address the other members of Blue Spark, Ava tried to lighten the mood: "You girls ready to rock?"

In response, Jocelyn played a New Order bass line and shook

her hair so it covered her face.

Doors were in fifteen minutes. The club set aside roughly a third of that for Blue Spark to soundcheck. The sound man's voice came over the PA. "Kick drum first, then snare, then the whole kit please."

Charlie was happy to oblige, leading with the hi-hat and pounding out a heavy boom-crack-boom-boom-crack beat. The sound of Charlie's drums in that cavernous room was like thunder and mud. Muddy thunder, maybe? Well, thought Ava, The Echo certainly lived up to its name.

"Guitar, what do you want in your monitor?" asked the sound guy.

Ava could barely hear herself up there but didn't know how to articulate her needs to the soundman. Instead, she gave a quick "I'm OK" and unplugged her guitar with a loud pop. "Sorry!" Ava said, shuffling offstage to wait for their set time.

In the green room, the three members of Blue Spark waited in uncomfortable silence. Ava always pictured bands horsing around and having fun before they went on. Was this what it was like for the Yeah Yeah Yeahs before shows? Tension and bad vibes?

Finally, Charlie spoke. "You little rock virgins ready to do this?" she asked. The question was rhetorical.

For Ava, the first half of Blue Spark's set was a blur. Lights flashed. Mics squealed. Mostly, it felt unreal—too easy, almost. From the instant they finished the first number, the packed room whooped and clapped. Jocelyn introduced a song, then Ava would do the next, just like they had planned for weeks in rehearsal.

A few tunes in and time slowed. Ava drifted far above herself, lost in the moment. A few times per song, she and Jocelyn looked at each other and smiled, but it was impossible to get their drummer to make eye contact. Charlie was playing directly to the audience, completely detached from the rest of the band, again behaving totally differently than at practice: twirling sticks, headbanging, doing the hair metal thing. It was as if Ava and Jocelyn weren't even there.

Charlie counted songs in at twice the tempo. After "A Dog's Dream," which climaxed with a dramatic guitar/bass/drums finish they'd been sweating over all week, Charlie began tapping out an unfamiliar pattern on the snare. At first, Ava thought something was wrong with Charlie's drums. Maybe she was tuning. What other explanation could there be? But Charlie kept going. And going. Building in intensity. That initial rudiment somehow turned into a five-minute unaccompanied solo.

"We love you Charlie!" someone yelled a minute in.

"Charlie rules!" This came from an older woman in a Germs shirt at the bar.

Ava stood, hand on hip, and watched, like everyone else in the room. Jocelyn shook her hair in her face and stared at the floor.

Finally, Charlie finished to roaring applause. One more song. They finished with "Any Day Now." Ava looked offstage to her right and saw the next band: a bunch of neighborhood jangle pop kids called Stealing Daylight. They stood waiting in the wings, ready to claim their share of the limelight, the audience now primed by the openers. Ava thanked the crowd for making Blue Spark's first gig so kickass and hustled off, collecting her amp, pedals, and cables in a frenzy.

The Echo's green room wasn't much more than some wooden benches, a table with a container of iced beer for the Scarlet Letters, and a dirty mirror. It was empty. Ava figured everyone must have taken off for dinner. This made her happy. She needed a second to catch her breath, to process the highs and lows of Blue Spark's first half-hour onstage together.

Jocelyn was close behind Ava, and the two friends hugged spontaneously. After what seemed an hour, Charlie arrived, the woman in the Germs T-shirt from the bar on her sweaty arm.

"Nice one, ladies," said Charlie. "You're not babies anymore." She grabbed one of the headliner's beers. "Been a long time since I opened for anyone."

"I bet it has," Ava said. It came out pissier than she expected, but she continued. "I'm pretty sure people liked our set." She was building confidence now. There was no stopping the truth. "But Charlie, what was—"

Charlie jumped in, "Marla and I are gonna have a few drinks down the street, then come back for the Scarlet Letters. You know my girl, Marla, right?"

"No," Jocelyn said and extended her hand. "I'm Joss."

Marla looked around fifty-five, thought Ava, as she watched the green-haired woman slap palms drunkenly with Jocelyn.

Marla was more than a few beers to the wind. "Was my babe the shit up there or what? Best drummer in LA. Ever!" She and Charlie spilled out of the room and onto the patio. Ava could still hear them as they stumbled into the parking lot behind the venue.

Over a post-midnight breakfast at Brite Spot Diner, Jocelyn and Ava tried to make sense of their first show.

Jocelyn sipped her Diet Coke. "She made, like, no attempt to signal us at all and played everything so fast I could barely keep up. But the crowd seemed into us. I mean, they liked Charlie." She paused. "That's for sure."

A paunchy guy in ripped jeans and a denim jacket covered with punk band pins approached their booth. Ava thought he looked familiar, but he also resembled a lot of hipsters who wandered Vermont any given afternoon. Then it hit her. She remembered denim guy from the audience. She recognized his trucker hat with the PAC-MAN logo. Ava remembered debating whether it was vintage or Urban Outfitters, missing a chord in the process. She wasn't sure what to say. Luckily, she didn't have to.

"You played tonight, right?" the guy said. "I like that whole Breeders meets Bratmobile kind of vibe. You guys into K Records stuff too?"

Ava's ears perked up at his mention of the seminal Olympia, WA label, home to some of her favorite bands. So, denim guy wasn't totally lame, even if he came on a little aggressive.

"I work at Flyover Records. You two have awesome voices," he said sincerely. "But what the fuck was that thing your drummer started doing? Sounded like "Wipe Out" on meth." He mimed spinning a drumstick and stuck out his tongue.

OK, this dude's a little weird, Ava thought as she drowned her Belgian waffle in syrup. She took the first bite. So good. "Thanks, man," Ava said, mouth full.

"What are you called again?" he asked.

Jocelyn answered immediately, with an edge. "Blue Spark," she said. "Like the X song."

"Nice. I love X. Oh, if you ever need a drummer, I'm Saul. I'm not saying I'm Janet Weiss or even Meg White. But then, I won't do a corny ass drum solo and make my bandmates stand around, either." Denim guy left a scrap of paper on their table, bowed lightly, and returned to his booth by the door.

"I actually really needed that," said Ava.

Jocelyn nodded. "Me too. Saul might be our first fan. It's pretty cool. I've seen him a million times at Flyover. Just didn't place him." She inspected the scrap of paper. "Plus, no one's ever approached us saying *they* wanted to play in *our* band." They ate in silence for a few moments, sitting with the impact of Saul's praise and offer.

"Wait!" Jocelyn nearly spat out her eggs. "What about Marla? Why have we never heard a word about Marla before tonight?"

"I had no idea Charla was a thing. Or maybe it's Marlie."

Ava surveyed the restaurant to make sure Charla or Marlie weren't holding court in some corner. She had no energy left for another surprise.

The girls went on like that for a good long while: laughing, eating, venting, two friends in a rock and roll band at a diner that wasn't ever going to close.

DRIVING DOM

Sam parked his Honda on Sunset near Vons, a few blocks away from Attila Tattoo. He'd paired his Black Dahlia Murder T-shirt with the baggiest pants in his closet, hoping to toughen up his image for the occasion. Sam wished he had someone—OK, a girlfriend with dyed hair and gauged earlobes—with him as he entered the shop for the first time.

Thanks to magazines like *Blasted* and *Ink Stain*, Sam knew that Junior, one of the best artists in LA, worked at Attila. The place was legendary for churning out high-quality work in a lowbrow atmosphere, but it was even scuzzier than he expected. The decades-old red paint was peeling off the walls in places, and the acrid aroma of brimming ashtrays spilled into the waiting room from the artists' area, which lay just beyond a wooden gate. Laughter punctuated by the intermittent buzzing of tattoo machines. The familiar whiff of antibacterial soap. Sam's stomach gurgled in anticipation. Junior, a bona fide legend, was less than ten feet away from him. The decadent thrill of the tattoo world never got old.

Right after his eighteenth birthday, Sam came home with his first one: a swollen-looking panther on his right shoulder from some place on Melrose called Dice and Vice. Despite considering himself a liberal Los Angeleno, his real estate agent father expressed disappointment. Sam's mom joked that it was her fault for taking him to see Blink 182 at the Grove in Anaheim.

"Most people with tattooed heads don't end up living in the Palisades," she explained to Sam. "Remember that." But their disapproval didn't stop Sam; the panther was just the beginning. As his collection grew, Sam took a job at FedEx in Studio City both to placate his parents and support his ink habit.

Sam did a lap of Attila's waiting area, taking in the yellowed flash sheets on the walls and plotting his approach. He'd saunter up to the divider and wait for a lull in Junior's conversation to interject some scripted trash talk. He knew exactly what he wanted: a classic dagger with a banner. Easy.

Before he could enact the plan, a gravelly voice called from behind the gate: "What's up bro?" Bald and burly, with two full sleeves of black and grey tattoos sticking out of his baggy white T-shirt, the artist introduced himself as Little Dom. While obviously Caucasian, his fashion sense was pure cholo.

"Let me see those tattoos," said Dom, bum leg dragging behind him, dangling cigarette dripping a trail of ash on the filthy carpet.

He grabbed Sam by his skinny arm and twisted it around, frowning at what he saw. "That one's alright," he said, pointing to a redheaded pinup girl with gravitationally improbable breasts on the opposite bicep. Dom was so close Sam could smell his aftershave. And he wore plenty. Once Dom released him, Sam shoved his hands in his pockets. The cranky host proceeded to demean one tattoo after another, insisting he could have done each better. "That supposed to be a swallow? Looks like a pigeon. I could fix that. What you wanna get done today?"

Sam pointed at a dagger on the wall. "I was thinking some-thing like that but with a banner wrapping around the handle."

"That's a stupid idea," Dom croaked.

Squirming now, Sam struggled to think on his feet. "An eagle with an eyepatch?" he offered.

Dom wasn't having that either. "I got a design for you. Something nobody's got. Come back here into Little Dom's area."

As he trailed Dom through the saloon-style doors, Sam saw Junior. He was a little guy in a Volcom sweatshirt hunched over his client's upper back, finishing off a family name in ornate lettering. Sam felt trapped behind glass. The pushy old man was ruining his shot at meeting the real talent.

Dom's station was a mess. Ink bottles lay on a silver tray like colorful, fallen soldiers. On the wall above them, a velvet painting depicting a dog card game shared space with dozens of overlapping stencils. "Check this out, bro." Dom pointed at a busy butterfly design which incorporated not one, but two pairs of female eyes into the insect's wings. The effect was hypnotic and unnerving but not at all what Sam wanted.

"Wow," he said. "That's really ... impressive, what you did with the eyes. But I was thinking of something different."

Dom disagreed. "Your buddies will trip when they see this. It'll be better than those poseur tattoos you got. Wait."

Before he knew it, Sam was in a vintage barber's chair and Dom was shaving his upper back, preparing to place the butterfly. The artist talked incessantly as he puttered around his lair, mostly jailhouse brags peppered with hints of submerged insecurity. "This Little Dom tattoo is gonna be the best piece you got ... I may have been locked up, but I ran shit on the inside ... I got so many girls ... I'm so ugly I'm good looking ... "

The weight of a muscled forearm on his back, the brief respite from the pain that came with each soap spray and wipe—Sam forced unwelcome thoughts of rough prison sex from his mind as he stared at the floor and waited for Dom to finish.

It took Dom nearly three hours to complete the tattoo. Halfway through, Junior and the other artists went home. Sam started to think Dom was intentionally going slow to keep his audience of one. It seemed Dom hadn't had a friend for a long time. Maybe ever.

As a teenager, Sam also struggled socially, preferring the reliable fantasy worlds of comic books and video games. It wasn't all that surprising he'd taken to body art. If Sam was honest with himself, getting tattooed was another way for him to collect rather than connect.

Sam shivered as Dom wiped the fresh wound down with a warm washcloth. Then came the familiar endorphin rush—the tattoo customer's version of a runner's high.

"That's the cleanest butterfly tattoo you're ever gonna see, bro."

"Cool," Sam said, looking over his shoulder into the mirror. Well, there was more green than he'd imagined from the uncolored stencil. And were the wings a little unbalanced?

As he left Attila, Sam saw Dom in the cramped closet preparing needles for the next day. The old man worked on his task with the quiet focus of someone who knew how to turn minutes into hours into years.

Sam's father was unenthusiastic. "Won't have to worry about looking for a new job anytime soon. Keep getting those things, and FedEx will be the only place that'll hire you."

"Well, it would be kind of pretty if the eyes weren't so creepy," said his mother.

Sam couldn't stop looking at the thing. Despite his initial misgivings about the design, he traced every minute detail of the healing progress. It got worse before it got better, that was for sure. The skin scabbed in places and peeled in others but finally emerged, like a monarch from a cocoon, in a form Sam deemed acceptable. He'd need another, though—a better one. And soon.

With the butterfly healed, Sam decided, against all logic, to brave Attila again. He would avoid Dom at all costs and talk only to Junior—it couldn't happen twice, could it?—but the wily gangster ambushed him.

This time, the old man launched right into a hard sell on a pricey snake design. Dom held a crumpled piece of transfer paper up to Sam's face. The snake had a magic-marker-weight outline and what looked like hastily applied decorative dotting on the scales. "No one has a tat like this, bro," Dom insisted. "Let's do it right now."

Once again, it wasn't what Sam wanted. The design was all wrong. Too blocky, too bold—even for a tattoo, an art form that valued durability above all else. Could he talk Dom into redrawing the image, maybe integrate a few suggestions? Unlikely. He considered turning around and running out the front door, but Dom hovered over him with his girth. Sam acquiesced and assumed the position, this time lying on his side.

The whole thing was over quickly.

Leg smarting, Sam consoled himself in the car all the way home. OK, even if he was the owner of another tat he didn't exactly want, at least it was a tough-looking snake. Hopefully, if he kept adding pieces around it, quantity would eventually outweigh quality. Though imperfect, Sam told himself it was a unique take on a classic; Dom swore the image was a one-of-a-kind.

A few days later, at the corner of Sunset and Vine, Sam saw a bike messenger stopped at the light wearing an identical design on his calf. No doubt about it. It was Little Dom's custom reptile. Sam sighed. He glared at his snake, which now looked even more juvenile. He wouldn't let that hack touch him again.

The experience so soured him that a few months passed before Sam let himself think about a new tattoo. Slowly, though, the itch returned. He even considered returning to Dice and Vice just to avoid Dom, but he still wanted that dagger from Junior. Sam decided to make a third and final attempt. He even called ahead to be certain Dom had the day off, but in Attila's outlaw style, the number was disconnected.

Once more, Sam parked his Honda near Vons and summoned some gusto as he walked to the shop. Again, he mapped it all out. Walk with purpose directly to Junior's station in the back. Bypass any distractions. As soon as he opened the door, however, Dom cornered him in the lobby, looking lonelier than ever.

"You know how the Pachucos lowered their rides back in the day?" Dom asked, getting right up in Sam's face. Dom answered himself. "Sandbags," he said.

Sam nodded. It seemed today's seminar was on custom car culture.

"You need to feel a lowrider, homie." Dom threw his bulky keychain from across the room. Sam caught the hunk of metal against his chest. "Today you're gonna drive Princesa." Dom ushered Sam out the front door.

Ground-scraping body, beefy whitewall tires, Virgin of Guadalupe-stickered back window, Princesa was both art piece and trophy, the vehicular extension of Dom's fixation with Latino style. Easily twenty feet, she was an imposing sentry. The yellow sunlight of Hollywood's golden hour struck Princesa's immaculate white paint job, creating a glare that was tough to look at without squinting. Sam approached the Chevrolet Impala with deference, holding his breath while taking in her full length.

"Go ahead, homeboy. Unlock it," Dom instructed.

Once seated, Sam gripped the blue and white leather wheel. Every detail—from dangling dice to analog mileage gauge—looked impossibly fragile. He exhaled, the sweat on his back plastering his T-shirt to the leather seat. Sam's hand rested on Dom's rabbit's foot, which hung passively from the ignition. Staring straight ahead in the passenger seat, Dom spoke in a cigarette-stained voice: "It's manual. You can drive, right?"

Technically, sure, Sam thought, wiping the sweat from his forehead, but the Impala was nothing like his Honda, a graduation gift from Mom and Dad. Dom flashed his gold-toothed smile. "I'm letting you ride my lady, homie. Don't be chicken."

Breathing in and out with great exaggeration, Sam turned the key. Beneath him, he felt the unfamiliar bounce of hydraulic tires.

"Nice," said Little Dom.

Lightheaded, Sam waited. Let them pass. Find an opening. Now. Merge. He pulled into the rush hour Sunset congestion.

They cruised down Sunset, soon crossing Cole, then Wilcox. The sun disappeared behind the Hollywood Athletic Club, then returned above the Money Mart at the corner, blinding Sam. He put on his sunglasses and sank into the seat. To the rumble of the Impala's engine, Dom smiled and bobbed his head. Sam tried to do likewise but was distracted by the afternoon traffic, the copious legroom, and Dom's always-threatening proximity.

Dom hung his arm out the window and smoked cigarette after cigarette. At first, Sam adhered perfectly to the speed limit, but as his confidence grew, he sped up a little, then a little more.

Dom glared. "Slow down," he ordered.

Sam returned the car to thirty miles per hour.

The ambient engine hum blended with Dom's rambling. "You never been in a car like this ... I tricked this bitch out ... when you go back home, you tell people you drove Little Dom's '59 Impala ... you say, I drove Princesa. They'll know what you mean ... " Sam wasn't sure who Dom thought he would tell, but then, Sam wasn't even sure Dom knew his name. They stopped at a traffic light. As they waited, Dom switched on the AM-only radio. Some oldie with lyrics about being a puppet under someone's command. Fitting.

"You like that?" asked Dom.

He knew this song from somewhere. Sam remembered Sundays in the car with Dad, hopping between listings all over Silver Lake and Los Feliz, occasionally even venturing past Western. His father usually wore a Tommy Bahama shirt and sunglasses and sang along loudly to Marvin Gaye's "I Heard it Through the Grapevine" and "Midnight Confessions" by The Little Rascals. His forearms were covered with thick blonde fur, bleached by the California sun. Sam imagined his Dad was a Hollywood big shot instead of a real estate agent. Maybe Dad couldn't teach him the difference between a V6 and V8 engine, but the years spent listening to oldies radio together had made Sam a repository of obscure music facts.

"'I'm Your Puppet,'" Sam offered. "Great song."

"I'm your puppet," Dom laughed. "That's fucked up." As the refrain repeated, Sam unconsciously inched the Impala closer to the Subaru in front of them. What if Dad drove by? What would he think of this? He wouldn't believe Sam could drive a cool car like this, much less know someone like Dom. The thought evoked the mixture of elation and dread he got in high school when he skipped fifth period to extend his lunch.

"Yo, watch it," Dom said. Startled, Sam sat up and slammed down on the brakes. The two of them lurched forward in the front seat. Sam hadn't noticed the lack of seat belts, but now, as he and Dom slid toward the dashboard, he realized their absence added to the spaciousness of the front seat, the sense of untethered freedom. Princesa slammed into the Subaru, restored headlights crunching on impact. Out of the corner of his eye, Little Dom was thrown around like a marionette, arms akimbo. His bald pate hit the inside of the windshield. Sam's head bounced off the steering wheel, and he bit his lower lip. Hard. The car stereo played on.

Sam sat up straight in his seat. Dom banged his hand on the dashboard. "What the hell, homie? You got to stay awake when you're cruising." He rubbed his head. "Fuck."

Sam gently turned the engine off and started to get out of the car.

"You sit down," Dom commanded. "Let me take care of this."

"Do you have insurance?" Sam asked.

Dom took off his glasses and glared. "What the fuck you think, man? Yes, I got insurance."

Drivers honked and passed them, brandishing middle fingers and disbelieving looks. Sam couldn't believe he was in this situation. His first car accident and it was in a gangster's Impala. As Dom exchanged numbers with the Subaru's owner (a young woman in a USC sweatshirt) Sam pictured years of indentured servitude, making needles in the back of Attila. Dom would call on him at all hours, demanding food from Vons, forcing Sam to clean ashtrays and scrub the shop's temperamental toilet. He would be forever tied to Dom by this mistake.

Finally, Dom returned and lit a smoke. Sam was glad for the facade of normalcy. "Start the car. I'm gonna let you drive but we're going back to the shop. Hang a right over there," Dom said without looking at him.

They drove back in silence. He was relieved to see Dom's usual spot still vacant, a massive hole no one was brave enough to claim, despite the paucity of street parking. Roy Orbison played in the background as Sam carefully backed into the space, hydraulics bouncing with every light tap on the brakes. Finally, the task was done. He had returned the bruised Princesa.

"Get out," Dom ordered. They walked in front of the car. She was a mess. "I gave you a privilege, homie. I let you drive my lady. What the fuck?"

Sam's throat tightened. He stuttered trying to get the words out. "I'm sorry man. I didn't even think I should drive but you gave me the keys. I'll pay you back. I have a job at FedEx."

"Bro, shut up. First of all, I *know* you'll pay me back." At this Dom pushed his sunglasses down his nose and looked straight at Sam. These were not the sad eyes of an old man; this was the icy stare of an ex-con who meant business. "Second, it ain't the money. I got so much fucking money. Look." Dom opened his wallet to reveal a wad of hundreds. "How do you think we got out of there so fast today? I gave the chick in the car you hit a grand, bro."

So that explained it.

"Dom, I know I messed up. Here, let me give you my number. I'll get all the money back to you."

Dom slapped him on the shoulder. "It's OK, homie. You're a

good kid. I know you didn't mean to fuck up Princesa. I got a buddy from the joint who'll fix her up for cheap. He owes me." Sam smiled hesitantly, warmed by Dom's unexpected turn but concerned about what "cheap" meant. (Not to mention the nefarious business for which a jailhouse pal might owe Dom a favor.) Sam flashed to a nightmare image of himself in his mid-forties, living at home and still working at FedEx to pay off his debt.

After slowly entering Sam's contact info into his flip phone, Dom dragged his bad leg up the steps to the shop. Before opening the door, he turned to Sam. "But don't you even think about stiffing Little Dom," he said. "I got your number, bro." Then he laughed and entered his lair.

In the front room, a twentysomething guy in a Dodgers cap pretended to study a dragon design. He had one visible tattoo: a bluish blob on his forearm. Dom was on the case. "Let me see that, homie. Wow, whoever did that really screwed up, no? Come back here. Little Dom'll fix that."

The customer didn't know what hit him.

Sam left them to their transaction and stepped outside. As he passed Princesa, an alternate version of events ran in his head: Sam splayed out on the white and green leather front seats, a newly anointed gangster cruising slowly through the Los Angeles traffic, his dangerous companion nodding approvingly. In this daydream, Little Dom was the ultimate accessory: a real live bad guy.

But this was reality. He kneeled before the alabaster goddess to inspect her disfigurement. Fuck. He'd really mangled the grill. Sam fretted for a full city block, again picturing Dom doing unspeakable things to him in defense of Princesa's honor. Then, as his plain, nameless Honda came into view, the laid-back swing of "I'm Your Puppet" returned to his hips. By the time he got in his car, Sam was wearing the whole afternoon—Dom, Princesa, the accident, all of it—like a fresh tattoo.

He almost forgot that he'd agreed to pick up the evening shift at FedEx. With a sigh, Sam turned the key in the ignition and pulled into traffic, welcoming the subdued power of his Honda. He opened the window for some air. The fading light of Hollywood at dusk felt romantic, fated. With a few hours to kill, he decided to stop at El Pollo Loco before heading to Studio City. There was plenty of time.

HAL AND ALLIE

Early December and the San Francisco sunset was giving Hal a good show. He enjoyed his daily walk home through these last blocks of the Mission, after disembarking the Richmond to Daly City/Millbrae BART train. He knew he was part of the problem—overpaid brogrammer staking a claim in this once Latino-dominated neighborhood—but brushed that thought away, instead focusing on the smell of chorizo and pastor in the air and the thick, burnt aroma of roasting coffee from the place that just opened. (Spinane it was called, and it was white inside and out, all white, just like every other new cafe in the city.) Soon Hal reached Valencia and 17th and the studio apartment he rented for $2,400 a month: par for the course in the city by the bay.

Hal was pulling his keys out when he noticed a homeless girl sitting against the freshly painted brick wall (again, white) of his building. She wore camouflage trousers and a hoodie covered in patches with indecipherable band logos on them. There were dreadlocks of at least three colors sticking out at various angles from her head: faded green in places, blonde-streaked in others, and finally, dirty brown at the roots.

"Hey man, do you have a few bucks for some pizza?" Next to the girl on the ground was a massive Bullmastiff. "I'm really hungry," she said and scratched her nose. There was a ring tight underneath her nostrils that focused Hal's attention and an odd tattoo near her eye—a little arrowhead or something. Her face was dirty, *very* dirty, with eyes a striking shade of forest green.

He'd never noticed anyone panhandling outside his building before. Hal had trained himself to ignore the parade of street people that populated the Mission. Keep walking and look straight ahead. That was his mantra. Despite his knee-jerk disapproval of vagrancy and the fact that she looked barely over twenty, Hal was drawn to the girl. There was something direct and confident about her. He wanted her approval.

"I have," Hal checked his pocket, "about three bucks in change. Will that help?"

The girl didn't have a hat or anything, so Hal dropped the coins in front of her and shifted his weight onto his other New Balance shoe.

She took the money and looked up at Hal. "Dude, of course. Thank you." She straightened her back and petted the dog. "Are you one of those tech dudes?"

"I guess," he said. "I work at Mozilla." That didn't sound very good. "But I don't, like, get wasted all the time and whoop it up out here like some people."

"That's cool," she said. "I'm just fucking with you anyway. I like computers. I used to play *Halo: Spartan Assault* all the time back in Salt Lake. Do you game?" She looked up at him with genuine enthusiasm. Like she really wanted to play.

That game was years old. Not the most contemporary reference point for someone younger than him. How long had she been living on the streets? "Yeah, *Halo* is cool," Hal said, feeling he'd been standing there at least five minutes too long, yet not quite ready to go inside either. He permitted himself a longer look at the girl's face. There was something feral in her profile, the way her jaw was offset a bit.

"I'm Allie. This is Rex," she said petting the sleeping dog, who stirred lightly and rearranged its legs. "We've only been in San Francisco for a week and it's already the best place I've lived."

"I better go inside," he told her.

"What's *your* name, dude? That's the polite thing to do when someone tells you theirs."

Hal wanted to tell her his name. The impulse surprised him. He countered it with a rational thought: homeless people were survivors. She knew where he lived. Wasn't that enough?

No.

He needed her to know his name too. Otherwise, their conversation wouldn't have meant anything, and Hal was deciding, second by second, that he wanted it to mean something. "That was rude. Sorry, I'm exhausted. I'm Hal."

Allie laughed. "Hal. Nice." An awkward beat, then: "I was just messing around. You're far from rude. I can tell. I *get* people, you know."

There was that frankness again.

Hal's stomach turned a bit, and he felt his ears starting to burn. "Well, nice to meet you, Allie. I'll, uh, see you."

He swung his laptop bag out of the way and pulled his keys out to open the door to his apartment building. He could do it by feel, barely needed to look anymore.

"Later, dude." She smiled and locked her green eyes on him. He went inside, reheated half a burrito, and played some dumb first-person shooter he'd got at Best Buy, every few minutes wishing he was outside talking to Allie. He paused the game a few times and paced the room, horny and lonely, her crooked jaw in his mind. When he went out an hour later for a carton of milk, Hal hoped he might run into Allie, but she was gone.

Riding BART the next morning, Hal replayed their whole conversation in his mind. What a sap. Of course, he'd never run into Allie again. She was too ethereal, too unique for him.

Just under five foot ten and a little husky, Hal was never the tallest, fastest, brainiest, or most talented, but once Myspace hit, he picked up HTML like it was nothing. His parents encouraged him to pursue programming, sending him to coding camps and after-school classes. Hal didn't mind. It was easier than trying to make friends with the jocks.

He looked down at the Firefox logo on his T-shirt. Hal usually displayed Mozilla's flagship product on a sweatshirt, shirt, or backpack, sometimes all three depending on the day. It's what you did in SF—like announcing your tribe. He tried to imagine Allie's street tribe. They'd probably laugh their asses off at him.

Hal liked eating lunch with Matt, a senior UX developer on his team. Unlike Hal, whose belly betrayed his sedentary job, Matt had the long, lean body of a Bay Area cycling aficionado. Most days, Matt shamed Hal with a description of his pre-work ride through the Presidio or a weekend trip up Mount Tamalpais in Mill Valley. Matt had a long-term boyfriend and was craggy but somehow preternaturally youthful in a way Hal associated with gay men. Sometimes, Hal wished he was gay. Their world seemed cleaner somehow, all white sheets and expensive jeans, friendlier than the emotional minefield of the heterosexual dating pool.

"I had such a crazy weekend," Matt told Hal as he took an Amy's Pad Thai meal out of the lunchroom microwave. "We drove out to Napa and just cruised around the whole afternoon stopping at wineries. It was blissville."

"Mmm," said Hal with a mouthful of Cup Noodles. "That sounds killer."

Matt took a bite of Pad Thai. "It was. Have you been dating anyone? I can't remember the last time you actually mentioned a girl."

Hal looked down at his Styrofoam soup container. He was used to this ribbing. Off the market for years, Matt seemed to get a vicarious buzz from nosing into Hal's romantic misadventures.

Sadly, there were few to speak of lately. He'd been going to work and back, then staying in and playing video games every night for the last two months, ever since that failed eHarmony date with Melissa. She'd driven all the way from Sebastopol but ditched Hal after the pumpkin flan and before the bill arrived.

"Not really," Hal admitted. Then he looked up from his noodles. "Well, actually, I did meet this one girl, Allie."

That night, he saw her at the bodega on the corner of his block. Allie was fishing around in her pocket for some change to add to the scattered coinage on the wooden counter. Next to the register sat a full carton of chocolate milk and a bag of Doritos. The East Indian man at the till crossed his arms and sighed. Allie wore the same outfit as yesterday, except the bulk of her dreadlocks were hidden under a Raiders beanie.

Hal took his wallet out. "Here. What do you need?"

"Oh, dude. Could I have like," she counted the change in her hand, "three bucks?"

Hal handed the man a few dollars and looked around quickly before adding a banana to Allie's purchase. "For some protein or potassium or something."

She laughed, and Hal saw some yellow teeth and a few sockets near the back where others had gone missing. He smiled back and put a six-pack of beer on the counter. Allie wobbled out of the store, tattered jeans dragging on the ground behind her. Do it, he thought. "Do you want to have a beer and play the new *Halo*?"

There was a delay of a few seconds, during which Hal pretty much wrote the whole thing off as a mistake. Then the skies parted.

"Me?" she asked.

Allie sat on his floor with Rex splayed out beside her. She and Hal had each finished two beers and their eyes were glued to the screen. Allie's shoes were off, and her double-socked feet stunk sweetly. She carried a thick fragrance with her already: a combination of body odor, patchouli, and dog. It was a scent familiar to Hal from the Mission, but not one he ever pictured inside his own home. It was out of place. Like someone had painted the room a new color and he only just noticed.

At the same time, his apartment felt cozier than he could remember. Allie's sweatshirt was rolled up to her elbows. Hal caught himself looking at the patchwork of pale crisscrossed scars and homemade tattoos.

"I look fucked up, huh?"

"No," Hal said. "Not at all." In the game, Allie shot one of his soldiers. "Hey, I thought we were playing together," Hal said.

"Sneak attack. I'm a double agent." Allie rolled onto her back and laughed.

Hal realized this was the moment. He wanted to kiss her but couldn't remember how to initiate such a thing. Instead he put down his controller, stood, and retrieved two more beers from the kitchen.

"What's the deal?   Are we stopping because you got whupped?" Allie yelled.

Hal handed her a bottle and sat on the beanbag chair. There were so many questions he wanted to ask her, about her arms, her hometown, high school.   He was better at responsive conversation but gave it a try. "Where do you and Rex usually stay?" It had sounded better in his head.

Allie sat up and flicked a dread out of her face. "Why? Can we crash here?"

Maybe he should have led with a question about her home life. Instead, he was confronted by the reality of the situation: that he had all but invited her to camp out in his living room. Beer. Video games. What had he been thinking? From the floor, Rex snored.

"We usually stay at the shelter on Dolores or camp at the park. It never gets that cold here. And I have a sleeping bag." She patted her overstuffed backpack.

"You can crash here," Hal said.

Allie unpaused the game and tossed the other controller at him. "Do-over."

After they played, he cleared out the middle of the living room. Hal couldn't fall asleep that night. How could he masturbate or watch YouTube videos in bed knowing Allie and Rex were camped out one room over?

At 6:30 a.m., he decided he had to rouse his guest and the dog. Allie was spooning Rex who whimpered lightly. Hal looked at her for a minute but started to feel creepy. He tapped Allie's shoulder.

She rubbed her eyes and sat up. "I'm going. I'm going."

"Sorry it's so early."

"I'm used to it," Allie said, flattening an errant dread. "We always leave the shelter when it's dark outside still."

They left the apartment together. Hal locked up and gave Allie an awkward half-hug. It felt oddly like the typical end of a date.

"Later, worker dude," Allie said with a smile. "Go compute."

Hal knew he was in trouble now. He was really starting to like her.

The morning at work was a shitshow. Confronting a massive deadline around a browser update, everyone on the team was acting aggro. For the most part, Hal didn't get too uptight about his job. No one complained about his work and he rarely ruffled feathers. He was a Steady Eddie and knew it: unlikely to come up with a massive breakthrough, but well-liked and reliable enough.

Rachel, an overworked full-stack developer who worked next to him, sighed so many times one hour that Hal thought he should say something. She was Korean and graduated from UC Berkeley, if he remembered correctly. They'd had a few nice conversations since she'd started early in the summer. Rachel came to Mozilla straight out of college and was a massive Giants fan. Hal sometimes imagined asking her on a date—dinner or a movie or something—but always chickened out. She had cool style (flashy Nikes and short leather jackets), and Hal worried he was too nerdy for her. Plus, what if she said no and they had to see each other every day?

Today, a new confidence emboldened Hal. "This deadline sucks, right? Anything I can do to help?" he asked.

Rachel turned to look at him, her brow furrowed, expression

disbelieving. "What could you do to help? We all have too much on our plates as it is." She turned back to her terminal and blasted out a flurry of code. "Why do guys always try to fix everything?" she asked of no one in particular, definitely not of Hal.

Hal's lack of sleep left him distracted, so he spent a few hours on and off searching forums for tips to improve his *Halo* skills. The thought of Allie and him playing again seemed idiotic as soon as it entered his mind. She was a street person— probably on her way to some other city or shelter or homeless encampment or something.

Still, he daydreamed about running into Allie again in front of his house, inviting her up, hanging out, kissing. He would help her get off the streets, clean up her life, eventually become his girlfriend. Hal envisioned Allie 2.0 in this future life, scrubbed up and healed up, just old scars and body modifications to hint at her past.

Around 4:45 p.m., he saw Matt getting ready to bail, already decked out in full cycling gear. This was on the early side of the unspoken departure time for the 9 a.m. crowd, of which he and Matt were both members.

"I'm so fucking ready for this ride," Matt said. "Today has been a bear around here. Everyone is being insane."

Hal was happy to see he wasn't the only one on the receiving end of what appeared to be a Mozilla-wide sour vibe. "Not so bad for me. But my neighbor was super stressed."

Hal went on to mention how Rachel snapped at him, but really wanted to tell Matt about Allie. He didn't know what to say, however. They hadn't gone out, but *something* had happened between them that seemed worth reporting. She spent the night at his house. This was unheard of in Hal's world.

"I got to hang with that girl I was telling you about," Hal said. "Allie. We had some beers. It was fun."

Matt snapped his helmet on below the chin. "Nice. Way to go, Hal 9000." That was Matt's pet name for Hal, which had forced him to do some Google research and eventually watch *2001: A Space Odyssey.* Matt lifted his super lightweight Carbonate bike from its wall hanger and followed Hal to the elevator. "What does she do again?"

Every Mission burrito joint Hal passed on the way home was packed. Apparently, gentrification had not yet ruined everything about his neighborhood. Mexican food still reigned, mostly because it kept high-paid millennials like him sated and happy. He chose a taqueria a few blocks from his building and took his place in line. When he reached the front, he surprised himself and ordered an extra carne asada plate. Hal told himself he'd eat it for lunch tomorrow, but knew he bought it for Allie.

There was no one outside his building, so Hal walked in the direction of the corner bodega. It was completely empty, save for the counterman who gave him an expectant look. Hal left quickly. He felt out of control, like a stalker.

You idiot, Hal thought. Allie told him about the park and the shelter and all that. She probably crashed at different people's houses all the time. Hal put his hand on the thin bag and felt the pleasant warmth of the burrito. It calmed him. He decided to walk a few blocks past his house to the park then circle back, scoping out a few other spots on the way.

It was around 7 p.m., and the Mission was hopping. Hal passed a hot dog cart and a few winos on a bench. He steeled himself and kept his eyes directly ahead. Jesus, what was Allie thinking living out here? In the middle of all this ... craziness.

He reached the park and saw a few homeless kids with the same kinds of black hoodies, patches, and dogs as Allie. They would know her, he thought. Or at least, they might. Hal spun his burrito bag in a circle, twisting the string of plastic dangling from his hand. He approached three guys who were huddled together talking.

"Hey, you wouldn't happen to know an *Allie*, would you?" His voice sounded reedy and desperate. One of the kids turned around and squinted at Hal. He had an unkempt blonde beard and wore a Thor's Hammer on a leather tie around his throat. The boy's face was dirty and his sunken eyes were filled with regret and a callow enmity. He stared at Hal with the same look of incredulity as Rachel at work.

"You mean, Allison?" the boy said. "From Utah?" He walked over to another group of kids and talked to them for a bit. Then he kneeled down and pet the dog that had been obscured by the wall of army surplus jackets and filthy hair. It was Rex. And attached to its leash was Allie, smiling.

She saw Hal and walked over. Against his better judgment, he offered the Mexican food which Allie immediately took over to her street friends. They ate voraciously from the bag. Maybe they thought he worked at a nearby restaurant and was giving leftovers away. He didn't care. Hal couldn't believe how happy he was to have found Allie. He'd begun to accept the likelihood that he'd never see her again, that their sleepover was a bizarre one-off.

Allie was surprised too. "What are you doing here?" she said, grinning, always grinning. "This is kind of like, *our* place, you know."

In a blitz of words, he told her he wanted to see if she and Rex were hungry and asked if she maybe wanted to play some *Halo*. He felt pathetic, transparent.

But then Allie's eyes widened a bit and Hal knew she remembered the beers and the warm apartment for her and Rex. He knew that she would come back with him. As soon as everyone had finished off the free food.

Allie's crew was protective. Hal knew he was an interloper: the one who didn't belong. Still, the aberrant notions they had about his intentions shocked him.

"Bro, she's not a hooker," the one with the scruffy beard told Hal while a massive kid with a Slayer beanie and pockmarked cheeks stared.

The giant spoke next: "Where'd you meet this lame-ass, Allie? We'll fuck him up if you want."

"He's cool," Allie said, standing next to Hal, placating the men of the village, these street warriors hungry for battle. "Hal's a gamer. We play sometimes."

He tried to look disinterested but beamed inside. The scruffy one muttered something and turned away.

The two of them walked back down 16th together, Rex keeping close to the right of his owner, occasionally looking up for reassurance before focusing ahead again. Hal asked Allie about her day and she told him that she had panhandled on Haight and got a bag of pot edibles that she would share. She didn't ask him about work, but he told her how stressful the atmosphere was around the office.

"See, it was meant to be that I got the edibles." Allie solved everything.

They reached Hal's apartment building and he opened the door at the top of the stoop. It was only the second time Allie had been here, but to Hal, the sequence of events had all the elements of ritual, a couple returning home. Some hipsters who lived down the hall gave Hal a look of mild surprise mixed with disgust as they passed on the stairs. Fuck you, Hal thought. I have a good job. This could be my girlfriend. What makes you so much better than me? But he knew. It was Allie: her oversize clothing and backpack, her dog, her odor.

He opened the door to his apartment, wiggling the key a little like usual, and lowered his laptop bag to the floor. Allie sat down and scratched Rex's head. "Do you have any beers?" she asked.

Thank god he'd stocked the fridge the night before. He sat on the floor with Allie and Rex.

"Do you know those guys, like, really well?" Hal asked, afraid she would reveal that one was her boyfriend.

"Just from the city," she said. "Except Joe, the crusty who was all overprotective and shit. Him I know from, fuck, I've known him forever." She swigged her beer with one hand and petted the dog's head in her lap with the other.

"Are you and Joe together?" Hal asked, a little too eagerly.

Allie looked at him and scratched at a dry patch on her cheek, evidence of the increasingly cold October nights. "Dude, no. What is it with guys always wanting to know if everyone's your boyfriend? No offense. It's just annoying."

Hal asked no more questions about street associates, instead wading into the comparatively safe waters of Allie's Utah upbringing. He wanted to hear about the person she had been and reconcile that with who she was now. As an offering of vulnerability, Hal gave Allie some background information about himself. Despite the job, apartment, and expensive sneakers, he wanted her to know he wasn't a total Silicon Valley square.

Hal described growing up near Sacramento, with its scorching blacktop summers and agrarian surroundings where he and his friends set off fireworks and drank King Cobra like the rap stars they idolized.

She told him about her parents: Mormons with a strict no alcohol, no caffeine regimen. Hal also learned that Allie dropped out of school at fifteen and that her brother had a wholesale T-shirt business in Provo. They didn't talk much, Allie said, but when things were really fucked she could call him. Her parents she had less time for—and the feeling was mutual. Though Allie wasn't so far gone that she didn't call on birthdays and Christmas. Even street kids had a sentimental streak.

They were both a little buzzed, laughing about childhood misadventures. She told him about getting left behind on a grade school field trip to Hogle Zoo and the guards finding her after hours outside the orangutan cage. Turned out her teacher didn't even call Allie's name in the lineup when the class boarded the bus back to school.

Hal lay on the floor, a hand propping up his head. It was 10:00 p.m., and he could barely keep his eyes open. That was the problem with beers after work: After the initial adrenaline surge, the whole day crashed down on him.

"Wanna play some *Halo*?" Allie asked.

Hal did not but sat up and picked up a controller. "Sure," he lied. They put in a few minutes before he paused the game and looked at Allie.

"Dude, *what*?" she asked.

"Can I kiss you?"

She laughed and put her head between her knees, then looked up and closed her eyes for a split second. "Sure. Yeah, OK."

Hal leaned in and put his hand on her arm. He felt raised scars and soft hair. Then he kissed her. She tasted earthy, like beer and camping and ChapStick. She kissed him back with her tongue and he became hard immediately. How long had it been since he had kissed a girl? There were a few dates that ended with some make-out sessions but always in a car or on a porch. It felt different to be in his own apartment, without the city as a chaperone.

Soon they were lying down and he put his hand up Allie's shirt. She wore no bra. Hal felt like he was in high school again, tracing the outside of Allie's small breasts with his hand, feeling her goose pimples rise.

"Dude," she whispered. "Dude. I don't do this a lot. Is it cool if we just rest or sleep or something?"

Hal sat up. He felt ashamed of his fast hands and the blatant erection in his Gap pants. "Sure. I mean, of course."

Allie turned around and pulled her sleeping bag out of her backpack.

"Do you want to sleep in my room?" he asked.

She smiled. "It's cozy in here." She pulled her shirt off. Hal looked at Allie's small breasts with their swollen brown nipples and the many homemade tattoos on her ribs and belly. One said SKUNX.

They climbed into the bag together and he held her. Hal didn't know what came over him, but he kissed Allie's neck lightly and said good night. The top of her back was moist with sweat. She smelled ripe. They slept like a couple, legs entwined, his hand on her warm belly. Hal bathed in a palpable sense of contentment he couldn't remember ever experiencing, one that began in his cheeks, collected in his sternum, and filled him up all the way down to his groin. He slept deeply.

The iPhone alarm woke him at 6:30 a.m., as usual. Rex was lying on his legs, a heavy comforting presence that made it difficult to get up from the floor.

"Allie, I'm gonna take a shower. Can you get ready to go?" He didn't know why he was whispering. Maybe because he didn't want to wake her at all. Covered by the sleeping bag, dreads spread across the beanbag they'd used as a pillow, Hal saw in Allie a younger version of herself, before the cutting and street companions and runaway life.

As he washed the Pert Plus out of his hair, Hal once more experienced that unfamiliar sunny feeling again. He struggled to identify it, eventually concluding it was the absence of loneliness. Allie was such babe, he thought. His kind of babe, though—not intimidatingly pretty or overt in her sexuality. She was the homeless girl next door. Hal laughed as he soaped under his arms. He wondered when Allie had last bathed and decided he'd delicately offer her the opportunity.

After showering, Hal put on jeans and his faux-vintage *Galaga* T-shirt from Urban Outfitters. The green logo and heathered material made him feel like a hipper version of himself. In the living room, Allie and Rex were exactly as he'd left them. The iPhone alarm rang on. Hal thought of the shelters and encampments where Allie's day routinely began. She must never get to sleep in like this. Hal laced up his sneakers and spoke to the still-dozing Allie. "So, if you want to crash out for a bit and then, um, take a shower or whatever that's cool. You can let yourself out."

She stirred and groaned without opening her eyes. "There's cereal and almond milk and stuff," he offered. Allie turned her back to him and pulled the blanket up to her nostrils. "Uh-huh," she mumbled from beneath the covers.

She must be exhausted from the constant struggle of the streets, he thought. Let her sleep. Hal closed the front door extra quietly on his way out.

At Mozilla, Hal wanted to send a mass email saying he'd slept on the floor with Allie. Who cared that the date began in the park with a bunch of street kids tearing apart his takeout burrito? That was merely the prelude which brought Allie and himself (and Rex, he smiled, couldn't forget Rex) together in his apartment.

For most of the day, Hal sat in front of his computer, working on a particularly buggy piece of code. Though his eyes were on the screen and his fingers tapped lightly, he was far away—holding Allie and feeling as alive and vital as he could remember.

A few times, Rachel looked over at him, and it seemed like she wanted to ask a question or say something but didn't. Hal chalked it up to his new unavailability.

He went to eat at Pier 23 Cafe (it wasn't that far a walk) and treated himself to a burger and a beer. He chewed slowly on a French fry and stared at the bay, at the boat tours heading out, heavy with tourists. He thought about Allie in his little shower. Though he'd never seen them bare, Hal could picture her legs perfectly. They were bruised and hairy, strong from long urban hikes. Allie would use his cheap body wash and stay in there as long as she wanted, stepping into the world baptized by the hot water, made new by the cool air that rushed to greet her in his apartment.

"Fuck."

Hal stood in the middle of the living room. In one empty corner was a hole where the TV had been. The floor there was covered in a thick layer of dust. The cable connector stuck out from the wall, obscene in its coiled impotence. The Xbox and both controllers were, of course, gone, along with Hal's entire video game collection.

He walked over to the kitchen. A box of Special K lay on its side next to an opened bag of Health Nut bread. Never a materialist, Hal was suddenly hyper-aware of exactly what he owned and how much of it Allie had taken. It couldn't have been just her, he decided. It was those fuckers from the park.

Inside the bathroom, Band-Aid packaging was scattered all over the sink. They'd cleaned the medicine cabinet out—even his migraine pills were gone. Hal laughed. Those wouldn't be much of a thrill ride. Maybe they ran little hustles on Haight Street, selling benign prescriptions as designer drugs to Marin County teens on the lookout for a weekend buzz.

The soft blue towel he'd picked out for Allie that morning was exactly as he'd left it next to the sink. Hal remembered thinking its inviting texture might appeal to Allie. He pulled back the shower curtain. The Pert Plus and body wash were in the corner. No one had showered here today but him.

He would go to the cops, Hal decided, but he wasn't ready yet. He had to think all this through. What would he tell them? He'd *invited* Allie into his home, didn't have her phone number or even a last name. What he'd been was naive. He thought of Allie's smile, her faded face tattoo, their conversation on the stoop that first day, the looks on the faces of her street friends, a dirty neck, nipples, Rex passed out on the floor as they played *Halo*.

He wanted to run down to the park looking for her, for the street punks, for his stuff. But he didn't care about the games and all that shit. Not really.

Hal crossed over to the window, passing through the empty area once occupied by his television. He widened a pair of bent

Venetian blinds. Dusk in San Francisco. Couples walking to and from trendy restaurants, a few derelicts, no one who resembled Allie or her pals. Hal wondered if she'd planned it all along. Perhaps this was a standard scam: Find a lonely liberal loser, charm her way into his home, then call in the muscle once the coast was clear.

He remembered the look Joe with the patchy beard gave him in the park. Hal read it as hatred or jealousy. He'd felt like a rival for Allie's affections. Now, in his empty apartment, Hal realized that Joe was searching his face for evidence of an easy mark. There was a canniness to that urchin which Hal hadn't admitted to himself. Until now.

Joe knew at the park they would rob him.

He and his pals ate the Mexican food he brought for Allie. Now they had his belongings which they'd pawn or sell for dope money. Hal didn't consider himself the savviest guy, but once he got it, he got it. He was lured by the bait. Allie hadn't even had to do anything particularly sexual with him.

Hal sighed and sat down. One beat-up beanbag remained, shoved against the wall, where the intruders had most likely kicked it out of the way during their lightning raid. Without standing, he scooted himself across the floor and pulled it over. Hal placed his head on the bean bag, wrapped his arms around himself, and closed his eyes. It felt good down on the floor. He could smell Rex, along with Allie's street stink, commingling on the bean bag, coaxing him into a fuzzy nap.

IT COUPLE

Scott and Sonja had been a bicoastal celebrity item for nine months, long enough to have had:

... four conversations about who was more famous: Sonja, the svelte twenty-three-year-old fashion design sensation from Park Slope or Scott, San Fernando Valley's own musical enfant terrible with the shaggy hair and plaintive green eyes

... code names for at least three substances illegal in both LA and NYC

... thirty-seven cabs to and from gigs, dive bars, art openings, and fashion week events

... six drunken break-up fights

... two studio sessions when Sonja sang backup vocals on Scott's acclaimed recent release (the producer buried her voice in the mix so only fans who read the liner notes knew she was on the record at all)

... one adopted cat they named Rufus after the disco band

Scott pulled at Sonja's sleeve and whispered: "Can we please go in the back? I'm in dire need of some Whitney." Tonight, they were in her town, drinking at The Salinger, a Lower East Side haunt recently renovated and reopened by Scott's friend Tim, a drummer with family money.

Sonja gave him a fake-disgusted look. "I hate when you call it that. Just say you are in dire need of ... cocaine." She whispered the last word, reached into her Louis Vuitton bag, and fished around, stopping with a grin when she found what she was looking for inside. "You love the cocaine, the c-c-cocaine," she said, laughing. Sonja did the last bit in her best '80s rock voice.

Scott hopped off the stool and followed Sonja to the vintage phone booth in the back that they used as their Whitney rendezvous spot. Sonja closed the door behind her and brushed Scott's hair out of his eyes. "You are so fucking sexy," she said.

Scott gave her a sleepy grin and kissed her on the mouth, tracing his hand down the back of her asymmetrical chiffon dress. It was one of her own designs, from the controversial Allah Cart line, with plenty of frippery and not a practical bone in its Holly Golightly structure.

Sonja pulled out a baggie of Whitney and poured some onto her palm. This was how they always did it: big, obscene bumps off her hand. Lines were for actors. Both high, they stood up in the booth and Scott grabbed her hands. He held them up above her head and pushed her against the wall of the booth, licking her lips with his tongue, swallowing the cocaine drip.

Scott turned Sonja around and began kissing the left side of her long neck while placing his right hand between her legs. "Easy there, tiger," she said and took his hand away. "You always get like this when you're high."

She straightened his denim jacket and kissed him, lingering, before patting him on the shoulder and exiting the booth.

Tim was pouring at the bar, so the drinks kept coming. Scott returned to his seat, holding court over a few bandmates and glad-handers while a Pandora classic country mix played in the background.

"The record is the best thing I've ever done," he said, throwing back a Whiskey Sour. "Sonja is my good luck charm. We just make each other ... better." He leaned over to the stool next to him and kissed Sonja's cheek.

She laughed and moved onto his lap. "Well, you're a fucking brilliant songwriter. I have to work a little harder at what I do."

A Patsy Cline tune came on, and Sonja began to sway. Inspired by the cocaine and the ache in Cline's voice, she moved to the dance floor, stretching her willowy arms out and twirling as colorful lights chased each other over her body. Sonja sang along, belting out the words with a preschooler's confidence.

Scott's current bassist, an oafish guy named Rex, snickered into his balled fist.

Scott, wired on Whitney, was on his feet, eyes flashing. "What the fuck was that?" Scott asked.

"Nothing, man."

"I'm not a fucking idiot, Rex. I saw you laughing at my girl. Sonja's a fucking artistic genius. What the fuck are you?" He pushed him with both hands, and Rex stumbled, lost his balance, and finally steadied himself against the coat rack. "When have you done anything original? You didn't even notice that I replayed all your bass parts on the record."

Rex had a good six inches on his bandleader and was very drunk. Without a word, he walked to Scott and punched him in the face. "Fucking scenester," Rex said as he ground the recent *NME* cover boy's cheek into the bar. Scott laughed as his face went numb, even more numb than the drugs had made it earlier. Under Rex's massive hand, he saw Sonja spinning in her handmade dress, still singing at the top of her lungs.

B IS FOR BEATRICE

I was there to audition for a guitar gig with Beatrice and the Bees. Since moving to Los Angeles from Cleveland, I'd done my time in cramped vans and dingy clubs with my old band, Cinder. But despite the sweat and effort, it just didn't happen for us. After a few years of surviving by teaching guitar to kids, I started selling copy machine toner in the Valley to make rent. It was a rotten gig. You cold-called businesses pretending their ink cartridges were low and sold them overpriced replacements. There were a lot of musicians in those places: toner rooms, they called them.

A drummer I knew from work told me about a semi-legendary singer who recently relocated to LA from the East Coast. I'd never heard of her, but that didn't mean anything. Even though I'd matured a bit musically since the Cinder days, I pretty much only listened to At the Drive-In and Converge. Beatrice's assistant—yes, she had an assistant, this was the real deal— emailed me three songs before my tryout. I dug in with the kind of stupid passion I reserved for life-changing opportunities. Beatrice's voice knocked me out right from the start, beat up in all the right ways. This was going to be my break. I knew it.

It was a perfect Laurel Canyon evening, all hyacinths and chlo-rine, when I knocked at the front door of the classic Hollywood home where Beatrice was staying. She was renting this place? Shit, she must have a real career. As I waited, I pictured arena tours with backstage catering.

A woman in a denim dress and chunky necklace opened the door. Laugh lines and leathery skin. Too many Malibu beach days. Based on my Google image search, I knew this was not Beatrice.

"Hey, I know you," the woman said in the kind of accent common to British expatriates in Los Angeles. "Didn't I see your band at Bigfoot Lounge or something? I'm Maddie, by the way."

"Great to see you again," I said, but I didn't recognize her at all. "We emailed, remember? Beatrice invited me to get together and try a few songs."

"Let me get B."

Maddie directed me to the living room, and ran up the stairs. With her cork heels and bare legs, she had a sunburned sort of sexiness. I reminded myself not to gawk. Don't fuck this up.

So I waited in the den for Beatrice—the mystery lady I knew only by voice. The room was an over-decorated, gothic hideaway with multiple sticks of incense and at least half a dozen scented candles burning.

"She'll be down in a minute," Maddie yelled from somewhere above.

I looked around. Knickknacks covered most surfaces and a grand piano occupied an entire corner of the room. There was a vintage typewriter, a magnifying glass suspended from the ceiling by a bronze wire, and at least half a dozen sloppy impressionistic paintings. The incense began to make me dizzy, so I sat on a green velvet couch and crossed my legs in a self-conscious Keith Richards pose. I tapped my foot and waited.

A half-hour later, wearing sunglasses and a snug paisley dress, Beatrice appeared at the top of the stairs, jet-black hair piled high on her head. In contrast to Maddie's weathered party-girl, B was pale and nocturnal in the classic rock star mode. Topped off by a thick gauze of burgundy lipstick, the effect was otherworldly. It was tough to determine her age—I think that was the point—but I placed B in her mid-to-late forties.

Beatrice floated down the stairs and into the room. "Oh good, you're not hideous," she said. Shock. Her voice was pure Jersey. "Maddie sent you the songs, right?" With her back to me, Beatrice slinked over to a vintage tin side table and turned over a snow globe in her hands.

I pulled my Martin acoustic out of its case and tuned up.

"You ready? Taking you fucking long enough."

She caught me off guard, and I fumbled as I tightened my capo on the second fret. "Want to do 'Endgame,' the waltzy one?" I stammered.

"Maddie sent you *that* piece of shit song? Let's do 'Children's Hour.'"

OK, no capo. Beatrice was demanding, but I figured she'd earned it with her lengthy discography and all that critical praise. I fingerpicked the opening figure of the song. She kept her back to me as she sang, that raw, expressive voice filling the den. It was stunning. I'd never played with a singer like her before. I held my breath and didn't miss a change.

"You're pretty fucking good, you know that?"

I had the job.

That was how I became Beatrice's musical servant, her on-call fixer for last minute gigs. I learned quickly that my audition was telling—Beatrice was always late for rehearsals. Also, there were no official "bees" in Beatrice and the Bees, just a revolving door of local losers often drunk, high, or unfamiliar with the material—sometimes, all of the above.

Our first show together was at the Troubadour supporting some recently-signed bunch of kids called Colorhaze. I'd heard their single on KROQ. It was actually pretty decent, not all that different than the shit Cinder was doing a few years back. But we aged out.

As I listened to Colorhaze's soundcheck, I felt a familiar jealousy boiling up. I forced the thoughts down with rationalizations: I was a professional, this was a new phase of my career— any horseshit to distract me from the fact that I wasn't up there fronting my own band.

We were meant to go on in less than an hour and still no Beatrice. When she showed up at the Troubadour, we were already onstage tuning and she was already little drunk. We started the first song and B staggered around the stage. If this was how she was going to act during gigs, I might have to quit immediately after the show, I told myself.

Then Beatrice began to sing and again I was smitten. That scratchy, inviting voice—part Chrissie Hynde, part Janis Joplin—melted me. All at once, I forgave her bad behavior. Supporting a real artist gave me purpose, distinction. B's talent protected me. I was a goddamn professional sideman. Take that, Colorhaze.

I was lost in the moment when B ambled over and yelled in my ear, her breath stinking of wine and cigarettes. "You're playing too fucking slow," she said.

I signaled to the drummer to bring the tempo up.

Two songs later, she was on me again. "Take a solo, for God's sake. They're bored as shit out there. And what is up with those head-bobbing moves? Quit it." Channeling some anger, I dug deep and played the hammiest lead I could, really emoting for the cheap seats.

By the time we reached the end of our set, even the Colorhaze members were watching from the side of the stage. We finished to enthusiastic applause. As I packed up, Beatrice complained that the band was awful and sacked everyone but me.

"Sean, come with me, honey," she slurred. "I want you to meet some people."

We walked into the audience, and Beatrice introduced me to an actor I recognized from an HBO series, a '70s rock producer who had worked with Aerosmith, and an infamous Hollywood restaurant mogul.

"This is Sean, my new guitarist. Wasn't he brilliant tonight?"

Her entourage loved the show. Without removing his trademark sunglasses, the producer even made special mention of my extended guitar solo. I beamed, lapping up the praise. So that's how we were gonna do it, I thought. She'd ride me onstage but play nice afterward.

The next day, B had me rehire most of the band.

At first, I couldn't figure out how Beatrice maintained her iconic status. It had been years since her last record, and that one sank without a trace. The answer was simple: Show everyone a good time all the time. B taught me that the most effective way to meet famous folk and make connections was to throw the best parties. And she did: lavish, catered affairs with open bars.

For B, one of the benefits of hosting was getting to play, so she always had me bring a guitar to her get-togethers. It wasn't so bad. Everyone knew me as B's accompanist, so at least I had a role to play in the proceedings. Truthfully, I enjoyed her Hollywood shindigs, even if things weren't as glamorous as they appeared on the surface.

At a Valentine's Day soiree, while waiting in line to use B's doily-laden Victorian-themed bathroom, I started a conversation with a happening indie actress. All I could think of was the scene from a recent Sundance favorite where she took off her top. "So, how do you know Beatrice?" I asked the impossibly big-eyed star.

She furrowed her eyebrows. "Beatrice? Who's that?"

Before I could answer, I saw B swagger over, more than a little buzzed. "Sean. Sean! Come to the backyard and play a few tunes with me."

I leaned in, out of the ingenue's earshot. "Can you pay me a couple bucks?"

"You should pay me, honey. Mick *Donovan* is here. You can give him a copy of your old band's CD. Ashes or whatever you guys were called."

Ouch. "Cinder," I said.

I followed B into the backyard. She wasn't lying. The legendary DJ *was* in attendance, but he was holding court over a group of beautiful people. There was no chance of meeting the guy, much less slipping him my music. I stood awkwardly outside the circle for a few minutes, skirting the perimeter of his greatness.

B pulled me away from Mick's fawning fans, clapped her hands together loudly, then whistled. "I'm going to play a few songs," she told partygoers. "You want to hear some music, right?"

A few whistles.

We launched into our first number, just acoustic guitar and voice. B was a little drunk but sounded good. I looked around for Mick Donovan. Maybe I'd wow him with my playing and he'd want to check out the solo stuff I'd been working on the last few years. This was Hollywood. Anything could happen. As we started our second number, a cover of "Stepping Stone," I noticed Mick walking back inside the house, his arm around the actress from the bathroom line.

A little after 12:30 a.m., I called it a night. All the way home to the Valley, I fumed over the check that wasn't in my pocket. Par for the course in the wacky twilight world of Beatrice. Still, as frustrating as my employer was, I was starting to meet people in the business. That alone made playing with B worth my time. For a while.

I was teaching a bored eleven-year-old the main riff from "Seven Nation Army" by the White Stripes when B called asking if I'd assemble a band for a television performance in less than a week. It was a high-profile morning show, but B was all studied indifference. Personally, I thought she was just showing off.

"Fuck, I've played it so many times ... but the audience is massive."

Beatrice was impossible. I already knew that. But a chance to play on TV was hard to pass up. I sighed, preparing, once again, to hitch myself to B's star. "When do we rehearse?" I asked.

A week later, I was pacing the parking lot in front of a Ventura TV station. Beatrice was twenty minutes late. We'd muscled through our soundcheck without her, but I was a sweaty wreck. I stood with my eyes on my cell phone, willing B to call back, when the show's producer Ted—a curly-haired dude in a Lakers jersey—tapped me on the shoulder with his walkie-talkie.

"Where is she?" Ted sounded pissed.

I shrugged and babbled about how this never happens. Eventually, ten minutes before air time, I saw B across the parking lot, surrounded by admirers, wearing black overalls and a ridiculous pink sash around her waist. "The producer guy Ted," I said, "he's freaking out."

B glided by without looking at me, eyes hidden by shades. "He always does that. You can't take him serious."

The band was waiting inside. Seething, I picked up my acoustic. And. Showtime. The TV hosts talked to each other for what seemed like an hour until it was time for us to play. The group played two songs. I shook my hair and tried to act cool but felt this weird combination of stiffness and hyperactivity. Somehow, we got through the song without a major train wreck. Beatrice almost cussed on-air three times during her interview, but the hosts loved it. To them, B's Jersey attitude was an asset, a charming eccentricity.

As we watched the playback in the station's lounge, B mimicked the nervous funky chicken I had done with my neck throughout the performance. "Look at those white guy moves!"

OK, that hurt. I packed up my guitar. "Wait," she said, pulling out her bent checkbook. "I have to *pay* you, don't I?"

Everything changed after that TV gig. I no longer felt indebted to B, didn't return her calls, ignored the Facebook invites to events where I knew she would want me to play a few songs. I never told her outright that I was quitting—you couldn't do that as a freelance musician in LA—but I ghosted B pretty hard.

Months went by. The text I got was classic, short on details, ripe with the promise of a night not to be missed.

Big event this Saturday. Art crowd thingie off La Brea. So many people you have to meet. Bring guitar. Xoxo

Maybe I was lonely. Maybe enough time had passed. Maybe I accepted the fact that her celeb circles were intoxicating, that they made me feel like a star too. Whatever the reason, I decided to go.

I arrived to a debauched, boozy scene, a gallery packed with the usual socialites and friends of B's, of which there was an endless supply.

B ran over and grabbed my arm. "Sean, where the fuck have you been? Everyone's here. Let's play already."

There was a makeshift PA set up in the back of the gallery. A drummer and bassist we used to play with were already set up. Were they all waiting for me? Jesus, she only texted me like an hour ago.

B grabbed the mic. "My guitarist finally decided to show up," she squawked.

I had to admit, Beatrice's reputation preceded her. I looked out into the crowd and saw a guy from REM, an NBA player, this cheesy actor with spiky hair—Jim something—all entranced by the singer's charisma.

Halfway through the gig, Beatrice stomped over to me. "You're playing the wrong song, for fuck's sake!" It was just like the old days. Whatever. B was the boss and I thought we played well.

Right after we played, B told the band she'd have some money for us in a bit. Then she pulled a vanishing act.

The bassist scowled as he sipped cocktail after cocktail from the open bar. He was a starving musician like me. "Where's our cut, bandleader?" he asked.

I texted Beatrice. *Where are you? I have to head out.* I drank my Rum and Coke and waited for a response.

In backroom. It's fuckn brilliant you should come back here

She had to be fucking kidding me. I told myself to be nice.

Early day tomorrow. Any chance of squaring up tonight and getting me and the band paid?

No money tonight. I'll explain later. Nightmare with the owner. Come to the afterparty xoxo

So it was going to be that kind of night. I was exhausted and wanted to go to bed. I told the other musicians I'd try to get our payment sorted out. Would they please give me their phone numbers and email addresses?

"This is bullshit. I played and I expect to get paid," said bass player, downing another free drink. I told him I understood.

I walked back to my beat-up Ford, feeling miserable. I'd failed my fellow musicians. Worse, I'd betrayed myself. Again.

The money never arrived. Big surprise. I kept teaching kids and trying to get a new band together with one of the guys from Cinder. Didn't think much about B or her glitzy parties for a long while. A year or so later, out of the blue, she texted me.

Are U around? Fantastic party tonight. We can do some old songs. Tons of people will be there bring guitar xoxoxo

I deleted the message.

GOLD RECORD

Bernard kneeled on the floor and unzipped the young man's pants.

"Look at that," he said.

The young man did not reply, but he noticed the way Bernard dragged the word "that" out using the glottal fricative. (The young man had recently learned the term from his vocal coach—one of the most expensive in Los Angeles, his manager told him.)

Bernard continued, undeterred. "Everyone talks about it," he said, now in a softer voice, like a second character of his own invention.

As Bernard's mouth closed around him, the young man focused on the wall of framed gold records. One day soon, his albums would share space with the giants up there. He looked down at Bernard's bobbing, bleached blonde head. Relaxing, the young man tried to imagine that Bernard was his high school girlfriend back in Omaha, then the barista with the twin lip piercings at Coffee Bean & Tea Leaf on Sunset.

For the last ten months—ever since he had discovered the young man at a Kibitz Room open mic—Bernard suggested that he wanted to fellate him. Just once. It was only fair. For all the work he was putting into jump-starting the young man's music career. Truthfully, he found his manager's come-ons flattering. They made him feel worldly. Like a star on the rise.

Not that the young man was homophobic. Even before leaving Nebraska for Southern California, he had a wild streak. Naturally rock star skinny, he always wore the tightest women's jeans he could find and applied eyeliner religiously before every performance. Plus, it seemed like everyone was a little gay in LA. Didn't the Chili Peppers make out with each other on an award show back in the day?

So as the advances persisted, he told himself Bernard was only maintaining his over-the-top, queeny showbiz persona. The young man went along with the teasing just enough to make the connections, secure the meetings, get his name out there in the LA industry circles. And Bernard had made good on all his grand promises, introduced him to A&R people and label executives. Besides, Bernard was a blast, always praising his good looks and commercial potential. Was receiving an enthusiastic blowjob from his lonely manager too much to ask in exchange for all this goodwill?

No, it wasn't. Bernard deserved this kindness. The young man grunted theatrically, starting to play along. "That's good," he said in his best attempt at a bedroom voice.

A few hours earlier, he'd been onstage at the Viper Room. It was a big gig for the young man, with at least half a dozen label reps in attendance. His girlfriend, Anne, even dragged a group of office friends to the show, to help pad the room. Under the flashing lights, surrounded by smoke from the fog machine, the young man couldn't see much, but he got a few glimpses of Anne. She had silver glitter around her eyes and was wearing a mesh top. He loved it when she came to his shows all decked out. In that getup, she reminded him of a young Bowie.

Sweaty, still abuzz with post-show adrenaline, the young man kissed Anne hard on the mouth. He and Bernard would be celebrating, he said. He'd call her tomorrow. After Anne left the club, they proceeded to down three Vodka Crans each before heading over to the La Brea office Bernard shared with his business partner.

They stumbled from the front door to Bernard's desk where they snorted some mediocre cocaine.

"No kissing," the young man told him and Bernard laughed.

With Bernard's hand around his cock now, the young man drifted towards and away from orgasm. He smiled, picturing his high kick at the end of the set closer, a new number called "Drip Dry." Yes, he'd been great, but the Viper Room showcase was a mere formality. The young man's band, Colorhaze, had already signed a contract with Virgin Records earlier that day.

He didn't have to pretend Bernard wasn't Bernard anymore; it just felt good. With his eyes shut tight, the young man pictured tour buses, guitar endorsements, late-night talk show performances. The future was wide open, yet unwritten, a blank page, and every other cliché. Bernard would take care of everything. He pushed deeper into his manager's mouth, thinking: I have a record deal.

CURE FOR LOVE

Reegan lay perfectly still in bed next to Darren, the first boy who had ever seen her without panties. He had his shirt off and smoked a clove cigarette. She couldn't look at him. Darren was too beautiful—that Nordic nose so pointy she could see up into it, his hairless eggshell-white chest.

"You want a drag?" he asked.

"Sure."

The air around them was sweet with clove smoke.

Remember this night, she told herself. You only lose your virginity once.

Darren swung around on the bed and put his feet on the floor. He grabbed one of his eighteen-eyelet Dr. Martens and pulled it over his black jeans, lank blond hair falling over his eyes as he laced up the boot. After summiting the first set of holes, Darren began working his way up the shoe's partner.

"You better get home," he said to the floor. Reegan was already pulling her Bauhaus T-shirt over her head.

Reegan loved Darren's boots; they were the first things she'd noticed about him. She'd been skulking around Smoker's Corner with the other goths at lunchtime. That day, it was Reegan, her best friend Siobhan, and the twins Raul and Jack, as usual, when this new guy walked up and asked for a light. She had never seen him at school before. (Weird, because she made it her business to know all the freaks).

Immediately she liked how tall and skinny he was; he reminded her of Daniel Ash from Love and Rockets. Reegan barely cleared five feet and was self-conscious about her middle, her thighs too. That's why she wore baggy shirts, concert tees mostly: the Cure, Lollapalooza, Ministry. Some were from shows she'd seen, others came from a head shop on Haight Street or the back of *Propaganda* magazine. She always bought a size large enough to wear over her tights like a dress.

"You have good tits," Siobhan told her once, applying eyeliner in Reegan's bedroom. "Don't hide."

Reegan looked at Siobhan, eyeing the toned body left over from years of gymnastics and Noxzema-fresh complexion. Easy for her to say.

Siobhan had only turned goth this year—she'd been a total muffy before that—but Reegan didn't hold that against her. Shit, if someone wanted to descend the social ladder to hang out with her crew of misfits, she wasn't going to stop them. Reegan was the one with the cred. Only a sophomore, she had started at Alameda High School as a full-on death rocker from the first day of freshman year. Her authenticity was unchallenged. This power dynamic was important to maintain between her and Siobhan. Maybe she wasn't as pretty, but Reegan had taught Siobhan everything she knew about Christian Death.

That day in Smoker's Corner, at the far edge of the quad, Reegan had been too shy to talk to the new boy.

"Where did you come from, mystery man?" Siobhan asked their lanky visitor. Poseur or not, Reegan was glad for her girlfriend's outgoing personality.

He raised his eyebrows as if to question who she was addressing. This, despite Siobhan's bullhorn of a voice, no doubt honed by years of gymnastics meets.

"Transferred. We just moved here from Nevada City. I'm Darren." Actually, he looked like Andrew Eldritch from Sisters of Mercy, Reegan decided, but cuter. She still couldn't say anything but gazed at Darren with her most entrancing stare. Reegan knew her eyeliner looked good—of that she was certain. She crossed her arms, then looked away, not wanting to appear too interested.

"I'm Siobhan." Of course, she won't introduce me, thought Reegan. Siobhan's extroversion was un-goth, and it made her look like a kid in a Halloween outfit. The dead air taunted her.

"I'm Reegan," she said. "I like your Docs." Then she turned and walked to fourth period, hoping he didn't look at her butt, hoping he looked at her butt.

Darren started hanging with the goths pretty much every day. He ate lunch with them and ended up in Smoker's Corner during passing periods. Siobhan tended to dominate most conversations, but Reegan occasionally snuck in a few words.

She stared at Darren's eyelashes, the faded cigarette burns on his right hand (a dare, he'd said), his thin lips. Mostly she talked to Darren about bands, but she did manage to extract a few facts about his life. He was old enough to be a senior but was repeating junior year and his family had moved on account of his dad's job at Lockheed. Darren got along with his parents all right; they didn't have many rules.

Unlike the rest of her click, Darren could blend in with the mainstream students. While the twins favored Dead Kennedys and Misfits shirts, Darren's white Hanes and black jeans were classic rebel fare. Reegan wasn't the only one with eyes for the transfer student either. Preppy girls decided he was the bad boy it was OK to like. Darren became a heartthrob, even with his crazy boots.

"New guy's a cutie," Reegan overheard in gym class.

There were rumors of him deflowering a few of the popular girls but Darren never breathed a word about these activities. When he was with the Creepy Crew—that's what Reegan and her friends called themselves—he was one of them.

But Darren had another life, on the upperclassman plane, that excluded Reegan, even Siobhan. Secretly, Reegan was intrigued by the tales of Darren's after-school dalliances that arrived through the gossip channels.

Reegan never uttered Darren's name; that would give away too much.

She and Siobhan were walking back from school, dawdling since only studying and MTV awaited them at home. Reegan kicked a rock with the pointy toe of her patent leather boot. "He can't really have done it with Maya, Esme, and that exchange girl," she said. "In one weekend? That's just gross."

Siobhan scrunched her face. "You have to be pretty desperate to do it with a guy at a party, especially one with a total rep."

Reegan didn't buy it. There had always been tension between the girls, but they'd maintained a tacit respect for each other. Siobhan's frank assessments of everyone and everything were exactly what Reegan needed sometimes. Conversely, Reegan knew her moody, critical nature, while exhausting, was couched in a loving protectiveness that made Siobhan feel safe. But ever since Darren's arrival at Alameda High, that once-unquestioned balance had shifted. They were rivals. And Reegan knew she had to act quickly.

Most nights, the girls talked on the phone well past midnight. Reegan's parents had recently gotten call waiting, but she mostly ignored the beeps when they interrupted their laconic late-night conversations.

That Sunday night they were chatting about the futility of Reegan asking for permission to see The Cure play at Shoreline Amphitheater in Mountain View the following month. The concert was on a Tuesday, making it an unequivocal "no" for her parents, whose idea of acceptable weeknight activities included little past homework, TV, and sleeping.

"I don't even care if I see the whole show," whined Reegan. "I can't be trapped in Alameda when Bobby is so close." Bobby is what the girls had taken to calling Robert Smith, the band's singer—he of the panda bear makeup and rat's nest hair.

Siobhan sighed. "Your parents are so tightass," she said. "It's one night. And it's The Cure."

Reegan hated when Siobhan complained about her parents, especially when her friend was right. They *were* uptight. Unlike Siobhan's single mother, who managed the JCPenney at Burlingame mall, drank a tumbler of gin nearly every evening, and listened to Laura Branigan, Reegan had a pair of normal, upstanding parental units. At home, they wouldn't let her wear her bat makeup, as they called it, so Reegan had to apply it on the way to school and wipe it off with makeup remover and pads before turning onto her block.

That Sunday, like most weekends, the whole family had gone to the movies and dinner at Coco's after. Secretly, Reegan liked these outings and her parents' basic decency. She judged Siobhan's mother for being too lenient, for letting her daughter wear stuff like the cut up Siouxsie Sioux shirt that showed her black lace bra.

The call waiting beeped. They'd ignored it the last time, which was at least twenty minutes ago. (How long had they been talking?) A sudden fear gripped Reegan. What if it was a work thing for her parents? "I better answer it," she said, then switched over. "Hello?"

"Is, uh, Reegan home?"

At first, she didn't recognize the caller as Darren. The juxtaposition of his baritone voice and the awkward greeting clearly intended for a parent, made him sound both older and more adolescent.

Then her stomach started to turn. "Yeah. It's me." Reegan waited a beat. "Who is this?"

"It's Darren from school. What are you doing?"

Her mind stopped. She felt woozy and a little happy. Darren was the call waiting. She also realized that he may have been—was probably—the one calling earlier. She had to get rid of Siobhan. He might call her next. "Hold on." She pressed down on the clear plastic ringer on the phone's handset, terrified it would hang up on Darren.

Reegan could hear music in Siobhan's room. It was "Tower of Strength" by the Mission UK. I need to get the tape with that song back from her, she thought.

"Took long enough. Who was it?" Siobhan wasn't patient on the best of days, even when she had absolutely nothing going on.

"Oh, it's for my Mom. Someone from work. I have to go." And like that Reegan told her first outright lie.

"Let me come get you. I want to see you," Darren said.

He'd never spoken to her like this before. This was actually the longest conversation Reegan had ever had with Darren. On the phone, he acted different than at school, almost whispering, but more talkative, more insistent.

It was the middle of the night, but Darren walked the whole way to her house. Reegan crouched on the floor of her bedroom, watching from the upstairs window. As soon as she saw his leather jacket shining under the yellow light of the streetlamp, she tiptoed down the beige-carpeted stairs until she reached the entryway.

Before opening the door, she looked in the mirror at her hastily applied eyeliner and black nail polish. She stretched her shirt out so it was further from her belly and caught a glimpse of Darren through the window. She had never seen him outside of school. He was even more perfect at night.

She walked over to where Darren stood with his hands in his pockets. She wasn't sure what to say.

He broke the silence. "Let's hang out at my house," Darren said, then turned and started walking. She watched the leather jacket move further away from view. He certainly wasn't making it easy for her to keep up. She caught up quickly and kept pace as they walked the three blocks to Darren's house. On the way, she provided the conversational cues.

"What did you do this weekend?" Reegan asked.

"Not that much. Went to a party."

"Cool. I just hung around the house, except to go to Tower Records in the city." She expected him to ask something about that, to be impressed.

Darren looked briefly at her. "Are you cold? You look cold. Here." He did not wait for an answer, instead stretching his long arms out and disentangling himself from his leather jacket, which he proceeded to place over Reegan's shoulders. She knew then that she loved him.

Unlike Reegan's family, Darren's parents were staying in a

yellow ranch-style home. It was a rental, he told her, while they figured out where to live.

"Totally," she said.

They went around back. Darren put his key in the door and turned the knob deliberately.

He motioned to be quiet and took her hand. Reegan's breath quickened and her eyes struggled to adjust to the darkness. The house smelled like bacon grease. It was packed with a surprising amount of furniture considering how recently Darren's family had moved to the Bay Area.

They crossed the living room to a door with a ripped *The Return of the Living Dead* poster. He opened then shut it softly behind them.

It was pitch dark, but Reegan could see Darren's translucent skin.

"Do you like me?" he asked. "I feel like you do. Sometimes."

Reegan closed her eyes. Yes, she thought. Yes, I like you, I love you, I love you more than Siobhan and all those preppy party skanks put together. "Uh-huh. I do."

Darren put his hand on her shoulder and followed it down her arm, then traced underneath her left breast, something no boy had done before.

"Do you want me to kiss you?" Darren didn't wait. He kissed her cheek, then her lips, and pushed Reegan onto his bed. A poster on the ceiling read: Metallica *Garage Days Revisited*. He continued to kiss her, across her neck and the top of her chest. Reegan realized she wasn't kissing back and started to make efforts to do so; this hurt her neck.

She looked up and saw Darren taking off his shirt, a silhouette until the moonlight hit him and she saw how pale and skinny he was. Then he was taking her shirt off and next her pants, kissing her chest, her belly, rubbing her breasts through her bra. She felt the blood rushing through her, tasted alkaline, got hair caught in her mouth, felt him pushing, pushing against her.

Something clattered outside the door. "Shit," a man's voice muttered. Darren sucked in his breath, struggling to suppress a laugh. He put a long index finger over his thin lips and mimed a hush sound. They waited. Reegan heard the ringing in her ears and the quiet of the house and the crickets in the yard. Then his fingers were inside her, too long and moving too fast.

"Can I?" he asked.

Reegan nodded and then it happened he was a part of her so close and pushing harder and she didn't move at all until he stopped shuddering and she felt his sweat on her forehead and her own sweat on her chest.

It hurt but it was over. Darren pulled off her and put a pasty arm behind his head. She rearranged herself and looked down at their four legs, lit slightly by lava lamp, side by side: hers naked and twice as thick as his black jeans-covered sprigs. Around one foot was her underwear; she didn't even remember him taking them off. She reached behind her back (which was sweatier than she could ever recall it being), and felt between her legs. When she looked at her hand, it was wet but even in the dark Reegan knew it wasn't blood. Wasn't that supposed to happen?

"I used a condom," came the voice beside her.

"I know." She had not known. "I was checking to see" she trailed off.

Darren turned to face her, putting a hand on his smooth cheek for support. "Your first?"

Reegan stared straight at the ceiling.

"Wow," he said, lighting a smoke. The sharp, piney smell filled the room. Darren was not worried about his parents making a surprise visit to the bedroom. Reegan pulled her panties up over her thighs and scooted into them, then flattened her skirt, still staring at the ceiling. She'd had sex with a boy. It didn't feel good like it looked in the movies, but it wasn't excruciating either. She had a strong urge to run home and call Siobhan, but of course, she could not.

"You want a drag?" he asked her.

The following day, third-period biology was particularly boring, so Reegan distracted herself by practicing drawing the Einstürzende Neubauten logo on the inside of the Mead notebook she used for lab figures. A few times, unexpectedly, she felt a slight warm tingle when crossing her legs and remembered the night before. It seemed impossible, like a scene from a movie.

Despite the time it took to put on his knee-high boots, Darren hadn't actually walked her home, just stood smoking as she walked off. At the back door, he'd said: "That was cool. I've been wanting that to happen. I hope you did too." He then kissed her half on the cheek, half on the mouth. He'd smelled sweet, like the clove cigarette he'd smoked afterward.

Reegan pulled out a black ballpoint pen to go over the Neubauten design again. Why hadn't she replied last night? Of course, she'd wanted it to happen. Just like she wanted to see him today and talk more. Maybe they would make a plan to go to Tower Records together or even into the city. Go to Haight. There were like five great goth stores there.

Finally, the bell rang and Reegan pulled on her backpack. She knew the quickest path to Smoker's Corner. One of the few advantages of being short was how easy it was to slink through the crowds in the halls. Her heart was beating so fast and her stomach was making all kinds of weird noises. God, had it done that last night? She told herself she would have noticed and rushed a little bit more, slowing down when she saw the black outlines of her friends.

The twins were talking to some kid she didn't know in a *TRON* shirt. Whatever. He was of no consequence to her. What startled Reegan was seeing Siobhan, looking every bit the perfect goth poster girl (she was such a lame), leaning toward Darren as he lit her cigarette. Her throat choked up and tears started to form. She took a deep breath and approached the group. "Hey freaks," she offered.

Siobhan blew smoke out of the side of her mouth. "Reegs. What's up?"

Nothing was up; she came here every day. What did she know? Did that fucker tell her? She looked over at Darren who was staring at his perfectly polished boots.

"Hey," he said.

"Darren and I were talking about going to The Cure with a few other people." Siobhan knew the impossibility of Reegan coming along. Somehow, her friend had a sense of what happened last night. Maybe not exactly, but she knew. The two of them kept talking but Reegan felt like she was underwater, their laughing voices never quite translating into words.

Darren didn't look at her. He laughed, puffed, stared at his shoes, flipped his hair, but addressed only Siobhan.

"I'm going to the bathroom you guys." She didn't even know why she'd told them. Siobhan said OK, but Reegan immediately felt like a total idiot.

She closed the stall door, put down the toilet seat, and sat cross-legged on it. Then she pulled out her Mead notebook and her black ballpoint pen, drew the same logo as before and a pair of Siouxsie eyes, and cried until the tears made the blue lines smudge.

Reegan didn't talk to Siobhan for two days before she finally broke down and called her.

"Hey."

"Uh-huh?" said Siobhan.

So she had noticed the disappearing act. "Some stuff happened last weekend," she began, "and I need to talk to you about it."

"I know you and Darren did it if that's what you want to tell me." Siobhan's voice sounded icier than Reegan had ever heard—older too. It made Reegan feel small.

"Who told you that?" Her voice quivered in that way she hated when she became emotional.

"Darren tells me everything. He doesn't understand why you tripped out so hard at lunch."

Reegan's stomach dropped. Now she was crying. "I wanted to be the one to tell you about it," she said, her voice choking. "Not him. I feel so gross."

"It's just sex," Siobhan said. "You're being a total baby."

Her dismissive tone of voice made Reegan's worst nightmare suddenly seem an unavoidable reality. "Have you? Did you … " Her voice sounded far away.

"What do you think, Reegan?" The phone clicked.

Reegan stayed away from campus the next day, skipping school to wander the aisles of the nearby Walgreens. Thanks to the auto-reverse function on her new Sony Sports Walkman, *The Head on the Door* remained on repeat the whole afternoon; she didn't even have to flip the tape. She drifted through the aisles, lost in the melancholy tide of the music. After an hour or so she didn't even feel like she was in Alameda anymore. It could have been Manchester, Oxford, London—any rain-soaked city, really.

She picked up *Tiger Beat*, a magazine she'd loved in junior high. She and her friends looked at copies together on the floor of her bedroom. Reegan realized she never talked to those girls anymore. They'd all abandoned her when she started painting her fingernails black and wearing what one called "Halloween crap."

Reegan remembered those days, pouring over photos of *The Dukes of Hazzard* and Rick Springfield in hunky poses. Now she shook her head at pictures of the new breed of Hollywood heartthrobs: Ralph Macchio, Emilio Estevez, Tom Cruise. They all squinted at the camera, pretending to look sensitive. Like Darren. They were all fucks. Robert Smith sang to her.

She walked over to the row where they kept the tampons. On the other side of the aisle were a dozen or so small square packages with promises like "ribbed for her pleasure" and "extra sensitivity." Reegan had taken health class twice, once in eighth grade and again this year, so she knew the importance of protection. No one wanted to be sixteen and pregnant, like an afterschool special—or worse: catch that AIDS virus she kept hearing about on TV.

Darren said he had used a condom. She even saw the wrapper on the floor of his bedroom. But she felt so stupid and dirty. It wasn't at all how she pictured her first time. The other night she'd been under his spell, but the way he blew her off at school the next day was mortifying. He had been inside her. She hated him so much.

She thought Darren was different. Quiet. Sensitive. But now

she knew better: He was a guy like the rest of them. Who even cared if he had great shoes? His taste in music wasn't even cool: mostly jock shit like Metallica and Guns N' Roses. Reegan bet the only reason he hung out with the freaks was that he thought goth girls would be easy.

A male clerk tapped her on the shoulder. Reegan pulled her headphones down around her neck. The metal band got caught in her hair.

"I said, 'Do you need help finding anything?' You couldn't hear me with those things on," the clerk explained.

"Oh no, no," Reegan said. She walked quickly to the cashier and bought three different kinds of gum. She felt lonely and liked it.

As she exited Walgreens and stepped into the parking lot, Reegan thought about her friend, the wannabe who didn't even know where the Smiths were from, or the difference between industrial and death rock, but who also made her feel pretty cool sometimes.

Then she pictured Siobhan laughing about her with Darren, and her throat began to constrict. Siobhan made it clear that she'd been sleeping around and had been for a while, bragging about exploits that made Reegan blush. Before Darren, Reegan had only kissed a few guys, mostly junior high games of spin the bottle. Reegan knew about the bands and Siobhan knew about boys. Neither one really cared all that much about what the other did with the opposite sex. Until Darren.

When she got home after her day of truancy, she decided she had to call him, tell him what an asshole he was. Reegan sat on the floor with her back against the bed and stared at the white plastic phone. It had a little chip on the receiver which had been there since she was little. She thought about the fact that she didn't really call boys. She'd certainly never called the boy who took her virginity. The knowledge that Darren would always be that boy made her sad.

"Hey, it's Reegan."

"I know."

"When I came over, I didn't expect ... I mean, I like you. I was surprised you even called."

"It's OK. Maybe we shouldn't have done all that. Are you cool, though?"

"Yes." She was under the spell again. Why wouldn't he ask her to come over? She'd do it with him again. She didn't care about Siobhan anymore. She would show Darren how much she liked him and they would become something serious, maybe not at first, but pretty quickly—

"Well, I've got to go. I have a buttload of studying to do. I'll see you at school, though." Darren paused. "Come to Smoker's Corner. Siobhan keeps asking where you are."

Reegan closed her eyes and pulled her legs up to her chest. "Siobhan said that?"

The next morning Reegan put in some extra effort before school. She sprayed the crap out of her hair and tried to do that Egyptian thing with her eyes. She hadn't seen Siobhan all week and wanted to look great. For her, but for Darren too.

Reegan half-walked, half-jogged from fourth period to Smoker's Corner where she saw Siobhan and the twins puffing away, actively ignoring everyone in her path. No Darren. She held her binder in front of her like a shield. She didn't care if Siobhan had slept with Darren, because so had she. As competitors for his attention, they were now equals. Siobhan couldn't treat her like a little kid anymore.

Siobhan raised her eyebrows. "Wow. I guess you're alive."

"Hey, Siobhan." Reegan looked down. Her initial bravery was fading. What did she even want from this? "I've been meaning to call you. I'm sorry. It's been a tough week."

"Bullshit. You don't like that Darren and I are friends—"

Reegan cut her off. "It's not that."

"Yes, it is that. You fucked a guy. That doesn't mean you own him, Reegan. I mean, you never even told me you liked him." Siobhan looked away and took a drag.

Reegan was crying now. Siobhan had never spoken to her like this. She wanted to run, but instead hugged her binder tighter, hoping it would somehow keep her planted there. "I never said that," Reegan said. "I just wanted to talk to you about it."

Siobhan looked at her with cool, inexpressive eyes. "You are much too immature for him, Reegs. Darren has seen a lot of stuff you haven't. I don't get all possessive with him. That's why we can hang out. You need to grow up." With that, Siobhan ground her clove out and sat on a decrepit bench.

For a moment, Reegan stood dumbfounded, processing her friend's utter and complete alienness. Was this what things were like on the other side of virginity, all mixed-up friendships, and boys who kissed you everywhere then acted like you were just sharing chem notes? The tears dried on her face in the November California sun.

"C'mon," Siobhan said and scooted over. "Eat your lunch with me. We're both adults."

Reegan didn't even bother wiping her tears away as she walked over, swinging her tin *Munsters* lunchbox. She sat on the bench and put her head on Siobhan's shoulder. At the crunch of Reegan's hairspray, both girls laughed and laughed.

TEST PRESSING

hey saul
no he's not here
uh-huh bunch of guys from flyover have been calling all day
zack owes everyone shitloads of money
that whole i'm an indie business mogul starting a label
thing was bullshit you know that right
i actually can't believe i lived with that asshole
everyone was like reegan don't be an idiot
yeah
i'm sorry you got mixed up with him too
of course i know you had nothing to do with it
you're one of the good guys saul
uh-huh
there was never going to *be* a record label maybe in his *mind*
you were giving money to a fuckin asshole junkie asshole
yes i know he showed you test pressings and contracts
me too
he said you were partners
guess what
i was his fucking *girl*friend
money from my drawer and *all* my vintage shirts
really rare ones my friend siobhan and i collected in high

school
    yup cure bauhaus mission uk the damned crazy valuable goth stuff
    stole them out of my dresser he doesn't even know most of the bands
    he only likes unlistenable shit like john zorn and ween
    oh yeah he is fucking gone he wouldn't dare come around here
    gone as in skipped town
    i don't know tuesday
    he's probably back in wisconsin or san diego or wherever
    yeah saul
    i'll call you if I hear anything

FROM DMITRI WITH LOVE

At 9:30 p.m., after a day of waiting for the enigma to appear, I'm certain Dmitri is a no-show. I'm a forty-four-year-old American producer in Moscow working with Ukrainian nu metal act TROL. The band's management hired me for TROL's first English language release, because they liked an album I did with Dizzjointed, a Milwaukee Limp Bizkit xerox. Not the highlight of my career, but now that every schmuck has a home studio, I take the paying work where I can get it.

My job in Moscow is to polish up the very Russian-sounding vocals at the center of TROL's harsh industrial din, make them a bit more intelligible. Despite the exotic locale, this isn't a glory gig. The money is decent, but TROL is more of a vanity project for its lead singer than a real band. Suffice to say, I'm anxious to get the ball rolling.

But first the singer has to show up.

In the world of TROL, Dmitri is the talent and the bank: a good-looking guy whose vague import-export day sounds pretty fucking shady. ("You know he's mob, right?" a session musician buddy warned me.)

I've been in country for twenty-four hours, most of them spent with the band's engineer, a long-suffering Belarusian with a ponytail named Serge.

"Dmitri, he own this whole floor," Serge explains as he shows me around.

"Impressive," I say. And it is, especially to a guy like me, hustling C-level gigs and renting in Sherman Oaks after a messy divorce. Oh, and whose credit cards are maxed out. I brought along the last one with room on it for expenses, but the second I tried to use the VISA at Vnukovo International Airport, my card company shut it down. Moscow must have looked suspicious to the call center in Duluth. Good luck trying to resolve the situation from overseas, especially with my cell turned off for overdue payments. When TROL gives me the second half of my fee, I'll sort it out.

On the plane ride over, I pictured myself staying in a swanky hotel in the city, close to good food and clubs filled with sultry Russian girls. Instead, TROL's management sent a driver to pick me up and deposit me at a hostel on the furthest edge of Moscow. I have my own room but share the floor bathroom with a Siberian wrestling team. After some observation, I conclude that these hulking guys are training at the rundown ice rink nearby.

Serge worships his boss' wealth, but Dmitri's personal recording bunker is pretty shabby: walls covered with carpet, hand-me-down gear, a large live room with a drum set, and posters of scantily clad women everywhere. It's a man cave where I can imagine Dmitri escaping to live out his rock and roll fantasy after a day of wheeling and dealing with underworld types.

Finally, around 10:45 p.m., the big man arrives—tall, muscled, swinging his bleached dreadlocks and sporting a perma-scowl. With his designer jeans and silver jewelry, Dmitri looks like a Russian member of Nickelback. On his arm is a young blonde.

"This is Olga," Dmitri says. "Serge, he know Olga."

Fine-featured and slim, Olga wears her hair in a high pony-tail. Olga—in her light blue jeans and yellow sweater—is an unexpectedly wholesome accessory to Dmitri's rebel aesthetic. The Ukrainian beauty smiles shyly at me but I avoid her eyes. I've seen mob movies. You don't stare too long at the boss's girl.

"Tonight we work on song 'Vampire,'" Dmitri says.

I sit in the control room with Serge as Dmitri butchers lyric after lyric. The man sings with immense gusto, but his pronunciation and pitch are appalling. Look, I've been doing this since the '80s and have heard some terrible shit. My studio bedside manner is a point of pride. This is tough, though.

"Dmitri, that was great," I yell between takes. "Can you say Vampire? Vampire. Not wampire. It's a hard v. Sounds awesome, though. Really rocking."

"Play again!" Dmitri yells, followed by a string of Russian to Serge. Serge laughs. Are they talking about me? For forty-five more minutes, the vocalist pushes himself in the vocal booth with diminishing returns. I continue providing constructive criticism, bookended by over the top praise—he is paying, after all. Olga sits in the corner, a beatific smile on her face, impressed by her beau's efforts. Look away, I remind myself.

Once Dmitri sings "Vampire" five times through with various corrections, he steps out of the booth to listen with us in the cramped control room.

"Da. Da." He nods his head to the playback. It sounds awful, but I figure we are on the first song of the night. Things will improve, right?

Dmitri leans over Olga and whispers under his breath in Russian. He then turns to Serge and speaks more loudly, punctuating himself by clapping his hands together and saying,

"Boom! Is good!" Finally, the mystery man stares me down with piercing blue Slavic eyes and says, "Tomorrow. I see you." Dmitri brushes his perfect dreads back and departs with Olga, like a real-life wampire.

One song. That's it for tonight. I can't believe I've been waiting around all day when I could have been out exploring Red Square, sleeping, anything.

It's late. I'm exhausted, jet-lagged, and without a working credit card. I tell Serge I'm going to walk back to the hostel. I want to get a little air after working on my studio tan all day.

"Nyet. It is not safe for you," he says, pulling his hair out of its ponytail, now clearly off-duty. "I drive." he says.

Serge is a good guy.

Back at the hostel from hell, the Siberians are joking loudly next door, letting off steam. I block them out by fantasizing about Olga. We are in the back of a limo, taking a night tour of Moscow.

You like this? she asks. At first, I think she means the statue of Lenin we just passed. Then Olga removes her blouse and pulls me towards her.

You know I do, I say.

The Siberians are still awake, partying at full volume. I ignore them and fall asleep feeling all kinds of guilty.

Today, I saw a bit more of Dmitri in the studio. His vocal stamina improved—meaning we got through more than one song. He came alone so maybe Olga's absence helped him stay on task. It was certainly easier for me to focus. Serge and I are starting to find our producer-engineer working rhythm. Basically, we humor Dmitri and get the best passes we can out of him, knowing we'll have to auto-tune his vocals later. Or get a ghost singer. Or both.

"My friend, what you wish to do?" Serge asks after Dmitri has left for the day.

I decide to be honest with him. The stale pastries and instant coffee at the hostel are not cutting it. "I am starving, man. Dying for a warm meal. The food where I'm staying is miserable. Can we go eat?"

Serge takes me to a dimly lit joint next door to a bustling bowling alley. I see couples out for a night on the town and teenagers huddled in awkward groups. Everyone is smoking. For the first time since arriving in Moscow, I feel like a human being.

It seems we're the only people in the restaurant not on a date. Serge tries to explain Russian romance to me. "You see those two over there?" Serge motions to a table in the corner where a black-haired woman in a micro-mini sips her drink across from a hideous gentleman with a comb-over.

"Is she a hooker?" I ask, trying to sound blasé.

"No, no. I don't think so. Man like that. He does not take prostitute in public. She is like girlfriend for him. Dmitri too has girlfriend like this."

This is my moment to ask about Olga and Dimitri. I have so many questions. For starters, she's way too young for him. Still, if her other options look like the oily dude in the corner, being mistress to the rich, comparatively young lead singer of TROL ain't that bad.

I try my luck. "Serge, buddy," I say, "you gotta tell me what's going on there."

"Well," Serge explains, "she give to him, Dmitri, two baby. He give to her apartment." He looks around before continuing.

"Olga is girlfriend. Dmitri has also wife and three more children." He laughs. "Too much. He is crazy. Me, Serge? No wife, no girlfriend."

On some level, I think I already knew all this but needed it spelled out. Olga is Dmitri's prize, a kept woman, waiting, much like myself and Serge, on the whims of the rock star.

Serge posits that to men like Dmitri, a mistress is a status symbol—illegitimate children a bonus, an extra display of virility. I begin to think Dmitri was showing off Olga to establish himself as the alpha male. This *is* starting to feel like a mob movie. I replay that first night in the studio and assign Dmitri new dialogue:

INT. RECORDING STUDIO - NIGHT

(DMITRI motions to the mixing board and musical equipment.)

DMITRI: You see this, American weakling? All this is mine.

(Gesturing to Olga with his thumb.)

DMITRI (CONT'D): And she, she too is mine! Hahaha!

I have much to learn about this strange, strange country.

The Siberians continue their daily training and nightly revelry. Serge and I edit and tune Dmitri's vocals every night after he leaves. I get a chance to call VISA from the studio phone and get my card working. Dmitri arm wrestles me between takes. I lose every time. Dmitri does push-ups in front of me. He says the same thing every time he stands up: "Boom!"

One night, Serge feels sorry for me being trapped in the bunker so many days in a row and takes me on a sightseeing tour of Moscow. It's not Olga topless in a limo, but I appreciate his kindness. Serge is solid. Somehow, by day nine, we've come up with a much-improved TROL record. You can understand a hell of a lot more of the words, that's for sure.

The day before I'm to fly home, Dmitri brings Olga to the studio to listen to the finished album. They both settle into the ancient leather couch. Serge turns up the studio monitors as loud as they will go. "The Reaper Always Wins" is the first song. It was no easy task getting the singer to make sure the keyword in the title didn't sound like "raper." That would start a whole mess of shit for TROL in English-speaking markets.

Serge stands and taps his foot. I pace and stare expectantly at Dmitri as the songs play, searching for any indication of his approval, waiting for the handclaps and the "Boom!" Hunched forward, his face obscured by dreadlocks, I can tell Dmitri is enjoying keeping us in suspense.

Then he cracks. He can't help himself. It sounds too good. In the middle of the song, over a massive drum break to rival even "In the Air Tonight" by Phil Collins, we layered three tracks of Dmitri's scream, one a perfect fifth higher than the others. The vocalist jumps up. "Da! Da! Heavy, man!"

The verdict is clear: Dmitri is pleased. I was worth the airfare.

Flushed with happiness, I risk a peek at Olga. She looks different tonight than on her first visit, older. In her lace skirt and strategically torn Bon Jovi concert T-shirt, Olga is dressed like she's trying out for the part of rock band girlfriend in an '80s sex comedy. I'm not complaining. She catches me staring and smiles shyly. I look down and pretend to bob my head to the beat of "Vampire." Am I crazy? Her lover would have me killed. Still, I like thinking she wore that getup for me, the hotshot producer from the States.

I don't need to worry; Dmitri is too deep into the music to notice my adolescent flirtation. As playback progresses, he gets more and more pumped, banging his head to the new sound of TROL and toasting the imminent worldwide success of the record. With the volume cranked, it's hard to hear everything Dmitri says, but I pick out some key points.

He is rich. Like, very rich.

He says I did "good job. Too expensive. But good job."

He lets me know that he "is more than just singer of TROL." He is "music video director."

And here I was, all week, unaware of Dmitri's other talent. He made a video for TROL. And we are going to watch it. After three more glasses of vodka, Dmitri screens the four-minute gothic melodrama on the studio computer. Olga is glued to the screen. I watch her watch him. Dmitri pays for her home, is the father of her children. He's the king of a self-styled kingdom. I am nothing here: a servant, the help.

"You like sushi." It is a statement, not a question. Dmitri is taking me out to celebrate the project's completion. I am weary from the week of recording and have an early flight to catch, but this is a big night for TROL.

Before we leave the studio, there is one last thing. Dmitri leads me up to his personal office and presents me with a rusted gold dagger. For a moment, I consider the possibility that we are to duel. Then I realize it's a gift. I am unexpectedly moved.

"It is my thanks to you. Very old," Dmitri says, his blue eyes sparkling. It's a cool artifact that would look great in my studio. Too bad there's no way in hell they're going to let me take it on the plane.

Dmitri's driver picks the four of us up and we stroll around Red Square before dinner. Dmitri points out the sights and I nod a lot, ignoring Olga at all costs.

As we walk, I construct a whole life for the two of us back in Los Angeles. We'll go to Universal Studios and Venice Beach. Cook for me? No! This is America, and in America, the man can prepare a meal for the woman. Olga, you'll never have to surrender your independence here. I'll help you learn English. You can study whatever you want, become a dental hygienist or a graphic designer, follow your dreams. The scars from my divorce will fade like the Cold War after glasnost. We'll inspire each other. My production career will pick up steam again. Clients' names will become more impressive, the budgets bigger. We'll go to the Grammys and Billboard Music Awards together and—

"Here, here is restaurant." Dmitri's broken English shatters the daydream. We sit and eat. The sushi is good, all the better because Dmitri is picking up the tab. I loosen up and joke around, even make a few feeble attempts at Russian.

Serge gives me a high five. "Great producer!" he yells, so loud it makes other people in the restaurant look.

Dmitri is happy. Olga has a calming effect on him. The two of them stare into each other's eyes and speak quietly in Russian, clearly in love. However misogynistic their arrangement looks through my liberal LA eyes, I have to admit it's working for them. Maybe I'm just jealous. I make peace with Dmitri, though I don't think he knows we've been at war.

"To fucking great TROL record!" Dmitri says, toasting with saké.

We clink white cups. "To new friends," I say. And mean it.

ILLUSION

"Okay, this is it. Biggest stage we have. It's actually the Guns N' Roses *Use Your Illusion* room. They rehearsed for that whole tour here."

"No fucking way. This is so sick."

"Yeah, I used to come to work the morning shift and see their roadies peeing in the bushes. I was like, 'Dudes, we have bathrooms.' Anyways, those guys are all cool."

"Hell yeah. I've loved them since high school."

"Me too, brother. Me too. Timeless songs."

"For sure."

"Anyways, you guys can use the big room today. No one has it booked. Just unload your gear through the side doors."

"No way. Sick."

"Yeah, your manager said Virgin is covering a lockout for a month of pre-production, so you're all good."

"That's cus the label wants us to put our music first. Because of our advance we can just focus on making the sickest Color-haze album we can. I'm so blessed, dude."

"Must be nice. Room B is gonna be your lockout for the month, but, yeah, what the fuck, use the big stage today. Knock yourselves out. Just no pissing in the bushes or any of that Guns N' Roses shit."

PERSONAL INVENTORY

Jim was a movie star with an over-tanned face—creased by the California sun and a decade and a half of abuse—much of it public. I remember the day Jim asked me to be his sponsor: He approached me during the fifteen-minute smoke break at a West Hollywood AA meeting, a trendy affair populated by motorcycle-riding rockers, film execs, and assorted hangers-on.

The whole experience was awkward. I didn't know what to tell the guy. For one thing, I was fifteen years younger and had never sponsored anyone. For another, Jim was a household name who'd recently starred in the first installment of an action franchise and was about to begin filming the second. (At least according to *Entertainment Weekly*.) I gave him a tentative yes, with the caveat that I would have to talk to my own sponsor.

"Don't matter in AA," my sponsor told me on the phone that night, adding that "age ain't nothin' but a number." What counted was sober time and quality of recovery. At sixty days out of rehab, Jim had little of either.

Then there was the whole celebrity thing. Despite AA's egalitarian philosophy, this was still LA. How could a plebeian like me give good, orderly direction to a millionaire?

We began meeting once a week, mostly at the Coffee Bean &

Tea Leaf on Sunset, a few blocks down from Fairfax. Over iced coffees, I learned Jim was fresh off a run that ended in a messy DUI. Jim needed something concrete he could tell the judge. He had an impending court case, so we made hasty progress through the first three steps of Alcoholics Anonymous.

Next was Step Four: the personal inventory. A lot of folks in recovery never make it past the first three because of the specter of number four looming in the distance. Alcoholics run scared from the kind of self-reflection this step demands. It's not pretty. That's why I was proud of Jim for pushing beyond the Step One, Step Two, Step Three dance and digging a little deeper.

When it was time to share his inventory, Jim invited me to his home. I couldn't even pretend to be cool about the summons. Admittance into Jim's world was a rare privilege, and we both knew it.

"Hey Matt," Jim said, opening the door. He wore a short-sleeved shirt with a flame motif and slip-on Kenneth Coles. Straight Melrose-wear. I decided that Jim looked better on film, where his chiseled chin, shirt-popping musculature, and spiky hair gave him an edgy, rugged appeal. Here at his palatial Beverly Hills estate, he seemed lost, over-styled for a Sunday, and visibly uncomfortable.

As he showed me around, Jim stopped to explain a few of his favorite art pieces, including a room of rare music and movie memorabilia. "I can't believe you have an original Raymond Pettibon flyer," I gushed, trying for a conspiratorial tone to bridge our economic divide. This was impossible. Jim had seen my one-bedroom apartment in Echo Park when he dropped me off once.

"Black Flag changed my life in high school," said the movie

star, with some sharpness to his voice. This was an attempt to impress me. I couldn't reveal I didn't have much time for Black Flag, and just smiled, nodding with enthusiasm. I respected the poster's monetary value more than its subcultural cachet. But then I didn't much care for Jim's film projects either.

His five-year-old twins—one boy, one girl, both blonde, a Hollywood staple, the result of post-forty IVF—played with Legos in the living room. Alex, Jim's orange-hued, botoxed second wife, prepared a smoothie in the kitchen. Despite the glimmers of her younger self (freckles, snug gym T-shirt, a pair of lightning bolt earrings), Alex's creaseless face actually *aged* her.

"Welcome, Matt! I've heard so much about you," she yelled over the blender.

"Thanks." I didn't really know what to say. I wasn't Jim's personal trainer. This was what you did when alcoholics asked for help. You worked the steps with them. And if they happened to be movie stars who invited you over, well, you got to see how the other half lived.

"C'mon man. Let's go in the back."

We passed through the kitchen's French doors into the backyard. I marveled at the detailed landscaping: swaths of spiral aloe and bunny-eared cactus jutted out between meticulously placed garden stones. Jim had bought this place with franchise movie money, the fuck-you kind. We sat on lawn chairs by the pool.

The sun was relentless, blinding, and as I put on my gas station glasses, I was keenly aware of their cheap make. The shades helped me get in character, and I launched into the same preamble my sponsor gave me. "I tell the guys I work with they don't have to be nervous. Even if you killed someone in prison, that's OK."

The line was there for comic relief and shock value. I mean, you rarely hear a murder confession in a Step Four inventory, though I'm sure it happens. The point was for Jim to know I wouldn't judge him. A sponsor is a keeper of secrets. Receive the dirt and hold your mud.

Jim looked down at the monogrammed leather-bound journal open in his lap. I strained for a glimpse at his upside-down scrawl.

"I guess I'll just start," said Jim and began to read from his resentment list. "There was my college roommate who told me I was a shitty actor. He never even came to the one-act festival I was in senior year. My brother for always getting Mom's attention." A pause before continuing. "And for being so good at soccer. My high school girlfriend, Tina, who fucked my friend Brian and lied to me about it ... "

He read on, and I nodded sagely. After a few minutes, the names became familiar: fellow actors, musician party buddies, his wife. The admissions were intermittently titillating (" ... then I started fucking my co-star's sister after the production ended ... "), but between boring passages about high school rivalries, I drifted off.

Jim looked up from the open journal in his lap. "Hey man, are you listening?"

I sat up straight and refocused on Jim. "Absolutely."

"I've never told anyone most of this shit."

After that, I listened closely and interjected affirmatives in all the right places, even a few wrong ones for authenticity.

We were an hour and a half into it when Jim started to sputter out, lost in a recollection about a shoot in Spain when he showed up hungover and mouthed off at the crew. "Let's check out your fear list," I said, trying to move things along.

Jim looked down. "It's pretty short."

"That's fine," I said. "Just give me what you got."

My sponsee stared at his journal. "I fear being found out, that people will realize I'm not meant to do this, that I barely even took an acting class until after high school." Sighing, he continued. "I'm afraid that the work will dry up and I'll lose this place." Jim waved his hand around without looking up from his writing. "I'm afraid that my wife will leave me and take all my fucking money because of this one set skank I slept with when I was working on that sequel last summer."

I peered over at the notebook, sensing some added editorial on the last entry.

"Yeah, I hear that," I said. "Anything else?"

Jim waited a beat. "I fear being normal, having to return to civilian life." Again, the running commentary. "I worry that I'll wake up and this will be gone, Cinderella-style, and I'll have to get a normal job."

I raised my eyebrows and folded both hands under my chin. I hadn't expected to hear disdain for the working folk expressed so plainly.

There, in the backyard, the truth confronted me: the elite didn't want to live like me any more than I did. Some actors clung to their salt-of-the-earth personas, posing as normal folks who just happened to accumulate a few houses and horses, but really wanted to live quiet lives. Not Jim. This guy was fucking terrified of losing his status, money, prestige, power.

Life was a fucked-up game of charades for him and me both. Difference was, he had the fame and respect I lacked. But he couldn't stay sober.

"So what spiritual principle is stronger than fear?" I asked him. "What would happen if you lost your career? Not that it would happen—but what if?" The discomfort I'd arrived with was gone. I was still, mighty, a spiritual giant.

I scanned Jim's face, a mask of introspection. He despises me, I decided. Sure, Jim wanted some kind of absolution he thought I could deliver. Mostly, though, this dude found me pitiable: my lack of VIP access, soft belly, simple dreams.

Jim grasped at straws. "I think I'm lacking serenity. I just want to be at peace." A pat answer.

I was unsympathetic. "Dig deeper. What's really going on beneath that?"

"I'm scared of being normal," he said. "I'm scared of seeing my family at Christmas and not having a movie I'm about to shoot, of being a fucking tool with no life." With those last words, Jim ran his hand over his bleached spikes, testing them for stiffness.

OK, Jim didn't despise me. He didn't consider me at all.

I stared a hole in my Vans. Jim's admission, so thin on self-reflection, so condemning of my kind, infuriated me. Don't look down on me, you philistine. *I'm* the one with the sober time, the college degree, the varied social group, and a haircut that doesn't look like *GQ* circa 1992.

I made my move. "You know what? That's a good place to stop for today."

Jim exhaled with relief, hopped up, and walked back into his perfect, superior life.

I asked to use the restroom. Jim's john was huge, bigger than my living room, with bamboo floors and unlit Anthropologie candles. I opened some drawers, grabbed a few ear swabs. Nice facial products, lots of lotions with SPF, very little evidence of the presence of children. A maid came to this house. Probably weekly.

I sat on the toilet and urinated like a kid who wasn't sure whether he needed to piss or shit. I considered jerking off, though I wasn't aroused, just to be perverse, to disrespect the room a bit. I flushed and washed my hands a few times more than necessary to negate my immoral thoughts. Be more spiritual, I thought. Jim has problems too—though not from the looks of this bathroom.

On my way out the front door, I told Jim to call me and we'd pick up his inventory next week. Happy to stretch my legs, I returned to my ordinary car and drove to a diner in the Valley where I was certain I'd see no one famous.

In my pocket, I held a movie star's vapid secrets. And, for a moment, that made me the powerful one.

SCENE STUDY

I was an acting student looking for a fix. During the day, I took classes in theater and set design at Santa Monica City College but outside of school my main role was rapidly declining junkie. I liked to think of myself as a damned romantic, guided by Stanislavski's ghost. I read Albee and Ibsen, but it was the method shit that really worked for me.

For forty-five minutes, I'd been wandering the Third Street Promenade, emitting signals. My leg muscles were spasming from dope sickness. How long since I'd last shot up?

Across from the Barnes & Noble, a dude panhandling responded to my street telepathy. His bushy beard and glasses made him look like a classic Santa Monica vagrant, but I knew he was my guy.

The air around him was thick with body odor. In front of the man, on his patch of sidewalk, lay an upside-down baseball cap and a battered backpack.

"Hey friend, anything going on?" he said. His hopeful expression encouraged me.

"Maybe you can help me out?" I exchanged a question for a question.

The man swiveled his head both ways like a western outlaw. "Let's see," he said.

Rising from near motionlessness, he collected his belongings and ushered me around the corner. I told him I wanted to score.

"You a cop?"

I pulled up my shirt sleeve and offered a peek at my ruined forearms. That did the trick.

"I'm Joe," the man said. And we were off.

Hands in pockets, back hunched, Joe led the way. We made a suspicious pair: college student in a Billabong sweatshirt and frayed jeans shuffling behind the panhandler, both walking with purpose. A nice, gray-haired Santa Monica couple hurried by, shaking their heads at our criminal partnership. My junkie roleplaying was working too well. Good citizens now crossed the street to avoid me.

So much great dramatic material. I made note of my co-star's lank hair and faded jean jacket, his mouth tight with concern, the gibbous moon and the evening's salty Pacific breeze. We talked in breathless blasts.

"You from here Joe? I mean, originally."

"No man. Midwest. Traveling forever, though." "Really? Cool. I'm in school."

"Caught a habit here. You know how it goes … "

I certainly did.

Joe deposited me at the bus stop. I felt a little superfluous, but as the solvent one I *had* contributed the capital. From my perch, I watched him navigate the classic steps of procurement: shifty pacing, head nod, casual exchange of goods, unassuming amble back to our meeting spot.

"How far to your place?" Joe asked. "I'm really sick."

"Me too. We're close, man. Just a few blocks from here, near the 7-11."

I felt a little guilty as we entered my ground level one-bedroom. My parent-financed apartment was far from fancy, but I did have a few amenities, like a television. Still, if my guest resented my relative prosperity, he gave no clue; that sagging face betrayed neither envy or antipathy.

Joe crouched on the floor and unloaded his baggage. My stomach turned over itself while I waited. I continued my scene study.

Dirty fingernails.

Composition notebook protected by a thick wad of rubber bands.

Sun-damaged hands.

Zippered denim bag containing his kit of junkie necessities.

Joe cooked down his half of our forty bucks worth of stepped-on black tar heroin (chiva, the Mexican dealers called it) in a spoon that looked like a Civil War relic. Next, he tied a faded leather belt around his lean bicep. Finally, with precise, practiced motions, he injected a syringeful of dope into the crux of his arm.

I tied myself off with my own belt and hit my forearm a few times to bring up a reliable vein. The little fuckers had become reticent lately, weary from overuse. When I got one to show up on top of my forearm, I pushed the needle in, swooning a little when I saw the blood bloom. Then it was all better.

Truthfully, though, for maintenance users like me and Joe, this was more like a morning coffee than the drooling lethargy of heroin cinema.

Now that we were both well, the two of us talked—nonsense, mostly. Drugs are a great icebreaker and we became chummy quickly. Joe had served his country before succumbing to the lure of the itinerant life. I served myself pancakes on a prepaid college meal plan, the good son gone downhill. Joe leaned back on his elbows, eyes softer now, less frantic.

"That's great … you're at school man … what did you say you studied again?"

"Theater … you know, acting … but there are … required classes too. English … science, stuff like that."

"Acting … an actor … wow … crazy … "

A glow of well-being in my belly spread to my toes, numbing them, inhibiting circulation. Joe's eyes closed for a long time and I worried that he might go out on me, but he eventually resurfaced.

"This is a nice place," Joe mumbled, before rubbing his nose and shutting his eyes again.

Now that I'd leveled out a bit, I was starting to feel uncomfortable with Joe in my apartment. The difference in our social strata became a pachyderm in my cramped living room. I had an exit strategy.

"Joe, you hungry?" I asked,

"Not really, but I'll watch you eat … actually maybe I am. For something little … "

I ushered Joe out the door and we hit the 7-11 where I bought him a King Size Snickers and a Big Gulp.

I explained I had to run lines for a scene tomorrow and bid Joe farewell. He made his way into the clear Santa Monica night.

Once he was gone, I did the rest of my dope and lay in bed making up a movie in my head starring Joe, kind of *Travels with Charley* meets *Basketball Diaries*. In it, Joe gets busted and cleans up in jail. When he gets out, Joe moves into a halfway house in Van Nuys, becomes a short-order cook, and meets a waitress with blotchy skin who wears too-tight Jordache jeans. She drinks socially and lures Joe out of sobriety. Within a few weeks, he's scoring dope again and hiding it from his PO. The climax of the film is Joe buying a bag from a guy who works in the kitchen, doing a huge shot in the bathroom after the late shift, and ODing.

I could hear the narrator's worn voice, someone like Harry Dean Stanton or Kris Kristofferson would be perfect: "For guys like Joe, time's passage was irrelevant. He marched toward oblivion in a straight line, an unquestioning foot soldier. Joe took life's lashings without complaint and his mind was a repository of wisdom."

As I fell asleep, I remembered something Joe said earlier. "You don't wanna end up strung out like me," he warned. "You got a lot going for you … I can tell."

PLAY THERAPY

Elon had been sitting in his psychiatrist's waiting room for fifteen minutes. His au pair Nurit always dropped him off early for his appointment with Dr. Bennett. Nurit moved to LA from Tel Aviv a year earlier and had been living with Elon's family the whole time. She was a big shopper and spent her free time during Elon's session on the 3rd Street Promenade. (Elon knew this because she always picked him up holding a new bag of shoes.)

At his feet was his backpack. Elon's homework had been increasing in scope and difficulty since he started fifth grade. He was supposed to work on it while waiting, but, as usual, the backpack remained closed and Elon played with the same toys he did every week in the yellow, windowless lounge. There were a few sets of checkers in crumbly boxes, a block game with plastic pins that particularly entranced him, and several buckets of green toy soldiers.

For the last three months, he'd been coming to see Dr. Bennett every Wednesday—ever since Abba and Imma sat him down and told him they were splitting up. The conversation hadn't come as a surprise. Elon couldn't remember either one ever saying anything nice to the other. The yelling got worse after Imma lost her part-time job at the library, something about cutbacks, which made Elon think of gardening. They never ate dinner together at home anymore like before. Now he went with Imma to the pizza place in Santa Monica or ordered Chinese food at Abba's office, where Elon's father was spending more and more time.

Elon was actually enjoying the extra attention he'd been receiving from both his parents since they dropped the divorce bomb. This happened to families on TV all the time.

At school, Elon asked his friend Meir what it was like when *his* parents split up. He and Meir had been going to Cheder Shalom Day School since they were in Gan together. A true opportunist, Meir had some practical advice.

"Chaver, you have to get your parents to give you gifts," Meir explained. "They feel so bad they'll buy you anything. That new video game you wanted? Ask for it. See what happens."

Elon followed the directions his friend gave him and found that Meir was entirely correct. It was as if he'd been taught a magic spell which enabled him to get all the things that had been in the past relegated to birthdays or Hanukkah. The more Elon asked for, however, the less satisfying the presents became. He found himself having more fun with the cheap toys in Dr. Bennett's office than his roomful of fancy ones at home.

At 4 p.m., on the dot, Dr. Bennett emerged from behind his impenetrable oak door and ushered Elon in with a mix of friendly brusqueness and afternoon exhaustion. There were many seats, but Elon chose the same corduroy chair as always, across from Dr. Bennett in his fancy brown recliner. The first week Elon asked why the office didn't have a couch like in the cartoons.

"So how are you, Elon?"

This was where it became complicated. After the first session, when they'd gotten the boring details of the divorce out of the way, Elon had been at a complete loss as to what to say to Dr. Bennett, who always had the same expectant look on his face. He didn't want to disappoint the old man, with his high-waisted trousers and hangdog jowls. "Well, do you remember those kids I told you about?" Elon asked.

"The ones who stole your football?"

There had been no such theft. "Yes, those ones. Well, this week, those jerks socked me in the stomach behind the school. They told me if I didn't watch out they were going to cut me here." Elon pointed to his Achilles tendon. "So I wouldn't be able to play soccer anymore."

Dr. Bennett raised both eyebrows. "I see."

Elon breathed out. Again, it was working. He continued: "Yes, they also said that if I told anyone they would *definitely* do it." Elon looked down at his hands in his lap. He made his voice to turn into a slight whimper for these last few words. He sniffed. "But I can tell you, right?"

"Of course, Elon." The psychiatrist moved in his seat, reached for a box of tissues, and offered them to Elon, all without taking his eyes of the young man.

"Thank you." Elon took a tissue and wiped his nose. "Take your time," said Dr. Bennett.

Elon tried to remember what else they had talked about the week before. It hadn't been a very interesting session. Some were better than others. Dr. Bennett always reminded him that he could say anything during their time, that this was all entirely confidential. The idea of an adult confidant was new to Elon who was used to reports from school coming home about his every misdeed.

At first, he'd been skeptical, but after some time went by without repercussions from his parents, Elon began to experiment. After all, there were only so many times he could describe how he felt about his mother saying his Abba had been schtupping a young woman from the car dealership and that she wouldn't be surprised if he was gonna try something on Nurit if she didn't watch out.

Experiencing a new freedom through falsehood, Elon told Dr. Bennett a story about a teacher who came to class drunk every day and one time made the class sit with their heads on their desk for the whole period.

Then there was the one about a girl who told him she knew a secret spell from ancient times to grant Elon anything he wanted if he kissed her.

Or the high schooler who had snuck Elon and his friend Daniel into an R-rated movie when they were supposed to see *Cars 3*.

He made up a real whopper about meeting Adam Levine from Maroon 5 at Baskin-Robbins and getting free concert tickets. (Sensing his self-made trap, Elon explained away the tickets as a birthday gift to a friend at school.)

The stories became more elaborate and less believable, but Dr. Bennett always nodded, asking interested questions at appropriate points in the telling. Elon became more confident with his tall tales with each passing week. Sometimes, he'd slip something true in to give them a layer of authenticity. A student from school would make an appearance in a fight or Nurit would scold him after some incident. His parents were conspicuously absent from the storylines, however.

Today, Dr. Bennett sat quietly and waited for Elon to speak. He always did this, and it made Elon uncomfortable. It's the reason why he started making things up in the first place. But today, Elon couldn't think. He stared at a poster on the wall advertising a Mozart summer series. It featured a stylized violin and conductor's baton dancing to invisible classical music. The image was friendly. Elon noticed the clock ticking; it sounded just like the one at school. There, he would hold his breath for as long as he could during class, just to pass the time. Elon didn't do that at Dr. Bennett's office. He didn't know why. It just didn't feel right. The silence was becoming too much.

"Why don't you tell me something?" Elon said. The words came out more quietly than he thought they would.

Dr. Bennett's face remained still while he uncrossed his legs. "What would you like me to tell you?"

Elon knew he was caught. He had no answer to Dr. Bennett's question. He'd merely been filling space. "Tell me why I have to come here."

"You don't have to come here."

"You know what I mean. Why do I see a doctor? Am I crazy?"

Dr. Bennett sighed and smiled. Then the silence again. "No, Elon. You aren't crazy. But you tell me a lot of crazy stories, don't you?"

Elon looked down at his hands.

"Your parents think you need someone to talk to about things for a while. Someone who can listen and maybe give you some perspective. But it works best if both of us tell the truth."

Defiance filled him. How dare this old man in plaid moth-eaten clothing call him a liar? His cheeks started to burn, and he thought he might cry. "I'm not a liar. You can ask anyone at school." Elon was crying now and didn't even care.

"Elon, I know you aren't a liar." He waited a beat. "For instance, everything you just told me was completely true. That's why you feel different. Your life feels different now, right? Without your parents both at home."

The young man wiped his nose. "I thought I'd like it," he said, fighting to get the words out between sobs, "but I don't care about extra presents. It sucks eggs. At least when they used to fight all the time we would eat together. Now, it-it's just me and Imma or—" Elon couldn't stop now. The tears kept coming. It felt good. He knew Dr. Bennett was listening and this was the honest-to-goodness truth.

On their way home, Nurit blasted the radio. She smelled like cigarettes and strawberry lip gloss. Nurit drove too fast, not like Elon's mom, who was so nervous she barely reached the speed limit, even on the freeway.

"What do you do in there?" she asked. Maroon 5 played on the radio. "Does he make you tell him your whole life story?"

The window was down, and the air felt great against Elon's face, drying the unexpected waterworks from his appointment. Nurit zoomed down the highway to the Palisades. Elon felt like he was in the Millennium Falcon. "I used to tell him stories. Now I tell him the truth. It's better."

She smiled at him. "Do you tell him about us going to get ice cream before your guitar lesson every week?" Nurit said and laughed. Elon's parent's thought he was getting chubby and didn't want him eating sweets, but she took him anyway. Sometimes Elon thought he was in love with Nurit.

"No." He looked out the window, lost in thought, a little part of him still worried about Dr. Bennett telling his parents he'd been lying. But underneath that churn, there was a humming— a feeling that told him everything just might turn out better than he thought.

DEPARTURE POINT

Wilhelmina slammed the hatchback door of her Ford Explorer (quickly, so the overstuffed camping supplies wouldn't spill out), took a final look around the parking lot of Trader Joe's, and breathed in some 8:15 a.m. Santa Barbara air.

Her electronic fob ceased functioning over a year ago, so she unlocked her door manually and sank into the fake sheepskin seat cover. It was still warm, despite the fact that Wilhelmina had spent over twenty minutes inside TJ's picking out just the right road snacks. (She hated the way popcorn always got lodged in her teeth and chocolate bars made a mess. In the end, only their Go Raw Trek Mix made the cut.) From the rearview mirror, a dreamcatcher dangled carelessly on a shoestring. It'd been there for years; Wilhelmina barely noticed it anymore.

She took a sip of her generic-brand canned espresso. So much cheaper than Starbucks and just as good. The first coffee of the day sent her heart racing but didn't make her jittery, just a little high. On this morning in early July, Wilhelmina was filled with a near-palpable sense of potential. The last moments before departing on a road trip were pretty special.

Pulling out of the parking lot, Wilhelmina turned the stereo up. It was a Medeski Martin & Wood CD she'd had in there for a few months now, since she and Ted broke up. He was the one who got her into that band originally.

She'd met Ted outside a Widespread Panic show her sopho-more year at UC Santa Barbara when Wilhelmina's dorm mate Sue introduced them over a joint. Only later did she tell Wilhelmina that the guy with the blonde surfer hair was her weed dealer.

Wilhelmina and Ted were inseparable that night: dancing, drinking, sharing more than a few hits of hyper-potent pot from a pipe Ted kept in the teeny pocket of his drawstring pants. After the show, they exchanged numbers.

For the next two years they were together. Neither one had to ask if they were a couple. It just happened. They didn't even change their Facebook status for like nine months or something. Junior year, Wilhelmina left the dorms and she and Ted got a place, though only her name appeared on the lease.

Wilhelmina was from a well-to-do Denver family. Ted was from Eugene, Oregon and barely escaped with his GED. Despite their class differences, they saw themselves as two hippies staying high. As such, they got along perfectly. Some of his musical faves, like those Medeski Martin & Wood guys, were an acquired taste for Wilhelmina at first, but quickly became a staple in their small apartment. So were Phish, the Dead, of course, and some old '90s rock that Ted's sister had turned him onto when he was younger. (Bands like Jane's Addiction and Blind Melon.) Wilhelmina worked on her Environmental Science degree at the University while Ted ran his booming pot business from home. They had friends. They had a cat. It was a good life.

She turned onto the freeway exit and picked up speed. The 101 North was a good straight shot, and Wilhelmina had no real destination in mind. This whole post-college hit-the-road thing was actually the first time she had allowed herself to enjoy the experience of not knowing since she and Ted had broken up. It had been two months since he hooked up with Paula, the yoga chick who worked the front desk at the dispensary.

You know I love you, he'd said. It's just that you're different now and I'm different now and things change, you know?

It's Paula, right? She'd made him confess that night which ended with Ted packing his three boxes of grow lights and Dead bootlegs and departing Wilhelmina's life for good.

At that thought, Wilhelmina ejected the disk and started flipping through radio channels until she found "Barracuda" by Heart. Perfect. She stared straight into her future. No more classes. No more Ted. He'd been her first college boyfriend: her first relationship, in fact. High school guys didn't count. As Wilhelmina drove, she realized she hadn't even left Santa Barbara since graduation. Most days, she'd preferred to hang around downtown, drinking coffee and feeling sorry for herself. The place was like a vortex of bad vibes.

A few weeks earlier, Wilhelmina was busy losing herself in a bookstore when she stumbled upon Cheryl Strayed's *Wild*. The book lit a spark. She'd already seen the movie, but still read almost the entire thing sitting on the floor of the bookstore. Something about seeing Strayed's story on the page felt like a challenge, a call to arms. She would have her own adventure, Wilhelmina decided, complete with camping and long solo drives like this one.

You know what your problem is? Ted asked her a few months before she outed him as a cheater. You know what your problem is? You never let anyone else be the hero. *You're* the one in college. *You're* getting the big degree. Because I sell weed you look down on me. You like me down here, Ted said. You get to be better than me. He ran his hand through his curly blonde locks, a few of which had colored string braided into them. He looked away. I swear, I read more books than you and I'm not even in school.

It was true. She had to admit that Ted was a true autodidact, filling up his free time reading everything he could. He plowed through Tolkien, Chopra, Dickens. It didn't seem to matter who wrote the thing as long as it was a paperback and cheap at the used bookstore. Wilhelmina could barely keep up with her assigned reading. It bothered her.

But today was her day. It wasn't about Ted anymore. It wasn't about her professors. She had her degree. When Wilhelmina checked her account that morning, there was a little over $1,200 left from her final financial aid payment of the school year, enough to cover rent and food for a few weeks while she traveled and camped. She'd keep it lean: Trader Joe's stops, peanut butter sandwiches, that kind of stuff.

It was misty out, but the sun was beginning to nudge its way through the cloud cover. It was going to be a beautiful California summer day. It was only 10:15 a.m., but she really had to pee. The next gas station couldn't be far. Yup, there went a sign.

Stepping out of the Ford, she took in the cool, salty air. She could see the Pacific perfectly from the gas pump. Walking a few feet away from the car, Wilhelmina pulled out her iPhone, took a selfie, inspected it, then took another with her head a little more to the left. That was better.

Out here, at twenty-two, on the road, her forehead acne didn't bother her, neither did the fact that one eye sat a little lower than the other. Ted never called her beautiful, but he used to say she had a great body.

Once, back in high school, she overheard a few boys calling

her and some other girls "butterfaces," meaning they looked better below the neck. She cried that night, even talked to her mom. Since her divorce, Wilhelmina's mother—no beauty queen herself—had been dressing in the same trendy fashions as her daughter. Most of the time it bugged Wilhelmina, but that evening, her mom felt more like an older sister. It was a pretty cool bonding thing for them.

You have a lovely face, her mother told her. And your brain is going to make you a hot commodity when you get to college. Just wait.

Wilhelmina still had to go to the bathroom but twisted and turned as she stood in place glued to her phone. She scrolled through filter after filter, finally settling on one called "Vista" and posting the image of her with the ocean in the background. Wilhelmina felt like Reese Witherspoon in the movie version of *Wild*. Hashtag: wanderlust. Hashtag: into the great wide open. Hashtag: freedom.

TAKE FOUNTAIN

I never set out to be a cyclist in Los Angeles, and I certainly didn't plan on becoming a teacher. They both just kind of happened. When I moved to Southern California from the Bay Area after college, my parents gifted me the family vehicle: a tan Toyota Corolla. The car was old but got great mileage. Plus, it came with a kick-ass stereo I abused prodigiously.

A few years ago, I awoke to find the Toyota—or rather, I didn't find it—fucking gone. The police recovered it a few miles away, stripped of all that could be sold. "Corolla Crooks," the officer said, the department's name for the criminal car club that heisted my hubcaps and the rest of the chrome. I took the insurance money, paid off some credit card debt, and—at the Costco in Atwater Village, right on the border of Glendale— bought a ninety-nine-dollar mountain bike. It's too hard to park a car in this town anyway.

My daily commute begins on the Eastside. I live near Astro Family Restaurant, a few blocks from the Silver Lake reservoir. There are actually *two* reservoirs in Silver Lake; both of them are fenced and inviting, mysterious facsimiles of natural beauty that serve as jogging courses for the hip, moneyed, and beauti- ful. I'm none of those things, but I dig walking around bodies of water.

Mornings and afternoons, I ride to and from my teaching job, bumping along with a familiarity that only comes from a daily ground-level commute. My route takes me up Rowena to Sunset, where Hollywood cuts in with all the subtlety of a cartoon villain. From there, I follow the advice of Bette Davis and take Fountain until I arrive at Highland Avenue and the bustling public middle school where I teach social studies.

Nothing like seeing junior high schoolers every day to remind you how righteously fucked life is at their age. Like many educators, I didn't exactly come into this gig with an insatiable need to mold young minds. Teaching was the only path to financial stability that gave me three months of paid vacation. This year, I plan to use those sweet summer days to develop my concept for an animated educational TV series.

Every day on the way to work, I pass the Nickelodeon building and imagine pitching *Dr. Hearty and the Vitakids* to the execs. The show is about a crazy bunch of vegetable children led by an awesome ringleader/mentor/teacher named Dr. Hearty. One kid has a cauliflower for a head, another is a plant with leaves for hands.

Each episode focuses on a different aspect of nutrition and includes recipes from around the globe, tying in each member of the multicultural cartoon cast. My friend Will is working on the artwork. I just need to polish up the pilot script. Nickelodeon will love it. It's a no-brainer.

I lock up my bike and sprint up the steps to my classroom, barely beating the bell. It's a punishingly hot April morning, and spring fever is in the air. With break a mere week away, the kids don't want to be there and neither do I. My first-period students look miserable. One in particular can't keep his head up for more than a few seconds at a time.

Bao is a rambunctious fourteen-year-old with jet-black hair he's always pushing back from his eyes. His first-generation Vietnamese parents own a convenience store at the notoriously sketchy corner of Santa Monica and Highland, just a short walk from the school. Falling asleep in class isn't too unusual. A few of his classmates have told me Bao is up until 3 a.m. most nights, haggling with hookers.

That's a rough life for a kid. Just the other day, on my lunch break, I saw two mannish prostitutes in a vicious, hair-pulling fight directly in front of the EZ-Mart Bao's family owns. Right now, I still have to play teacher.

"Bao, heads up, buddy!" I feel bad calling kids out in class. It's not like I wasn't a teenager once and didn't doze off while some blowhard teacher droned on and on.

"Sorry, Mr. T.," says Bao. (That's what the kids call me. I have to admit it sounds a lot cooler than Mr. Teitelbaum.) "I feel like crap."

The kids around Bao giggle.

"All right, all right," I say, steering us back to my Westward Expansion lesson. I'm worried about the sweet Asian kid with the floppy hair. He really looks like hell today.

During passing period, I notice a pair of boys huddled around Bao in the hall. He has his Hurley T-shirt pulled over his head. I push through the adolescent throng.

"Damn, Bao. That's fucked up," says Eddy, a good-natured jock.

Nils, a buck-toothed cut-up, laughs loudly. "Language," I say to Eddy.

"Look!" Eddy points at Bao's back. It's covered in rows of symmetrical red circles, all slightly raised and inflamed. The marks are turning purple in places. The effect is tribal, like someone tortured him. Bao looks like a "before" drawing of one of the Vitakids; Dr. Hearty would not approve.

"Bao," I ask, "who did this to you?"

"It's OK. It don't hurt," he tells me with a smile.

I raise an eyebrow. "*Doesn't* hurt. Let's be real, though. They look awful."

Bao pulls his shirt down and pushes back his bangs. "I gotta go, Mr. T., I've got Math."

Before I can interrogate him further, Bao speeds off to his next class. I look around for the other two boys, but they've moved on to different mischiefs.

I teach my second and third periods, shushing more rowdy kids during my lecture on the War of 1812, and administering a quiz to the eighth graders on the basic tenets of Communism. The whole time, I keep picturing those ugly, irritated marks on Bao's back.

Perversely, the Vitakids song is on loop in my brain:

Let's be happy with Dr. Hearty

We'll get healthy and oh so smarty

Even after lunch, Bao's back continues to trouble me.

Our district recently hosted a Mandatory Reporter Training, so the California bylaws are fresh in mind. I don't want to turn Bao's life upside down by getting Child Protective Services involved, but those welts didn't get there on their own. What would the real Mr. T. do? Or Dr. Hearty for that matter.

Fuck.

I sigh and decide to do a bit of reconnaissance.

The bell rings at 3:35 p.m., and I'm on my bike at forty after, pedaling the few blocks from Fountain and Highland to Santa Monica, where I figure I'll find Bao's mom working the tail end of the day shift.

I lock my bicycle up and remind myself to keep an eye on it. This parking lot is not a safe place to leave a bike, even a budget Costco model like mine.

Jesus, it has to be ninety degrees out. With my sweaty clothes and cheap sunglasses, I wonder if anyone will believe I'm actually a middle school teacher. Before entering the store, I make sure to wipe my hands on my pants and tuck in my shirt. I'm trying to project some level of professional composure, always a challenge after a bike ride through Hollywood.

EZ–Mart is hopping with locals trying to beat the afternoon heat. It's a small store, less than 200 square feet, but what Bao's parents lack in footage, they make up for in inventory. There's an ample selection of booze, cigarettes, and quick impulse buys at the register: Horny Goat Weed, Cadbury Creme Eggs, bumper stickers reading "Mi Vida Loca."

A group of kids from the nearby high school are horsing around and buying candy. One tries for a pack of Camels. Bao's mother shoos him off. Behind them in line is a middle-aged Hispanic man, just off work, who purchases three Lotería tickets and scratches them off immediately. The man throws them away and walks out.

I approach the register where a small lady in a yellow apron stands, arms crossed. "Hello, Mrs. Nguyen," I say. "I'm Bao's teacher. Do you remember when we met at parent conferences?" Remembering I need to compensate for my disheveled appearance, I offer my hand.

"What Bao do this time?" she asks, brushing something off the counter.

"Bao's not in any trouble. I came to ask about the marks on his back. Some of the kids were giving him a hard time."

Things get quiet for a moment. I script the phone call I'm

going to have to make to CPS:

My adolescent student is the victim of abuse at the hands of his family. He also works after hours at a convenience store and interacts with sex workers on a daily basis, but that's not why I'm calling. It's his back. It's covered with angry-looking red marks. When did I see this? He was showing a group—

Bao's mother begins to laugh.

I don't know what say.

She makes her hand into a claw and mimes an up-and-down motion. "That for taking care of cold. Bao sick." She softens—a little. "Cupping? You know this?"

Cupping. Images from herb shops on Haight Street and a post-college trip to Thailand flash through my mind. Bao's mother gave him a traditional Vietnamese treatment. I feel like a total asshole.

I exhale and fake-laugh, praying Mrs. Nguyen forgives my cultural ignorance. "Oh, I see. You were just treating him. For his cold."

Mrs. Nguyen turns her back to me and straightens up the cigarettes.

Now I feel the need to assert my validity as an educator. "Well, other than that one concern, Bao is doing OK." If I wasn't such a culturally clueless dipshit I'd mention her son falling asleep in class.

Bao walks in the front door. If he's surprised to see me he doesn't show it. Smart kid. He's perceptive enough to figure out the reason for my impromptu bike-by.

"Mr. T., my mom she told you I'm OK, right? We always do it when we get sick." Bao smiles and slides around the candy to get behind the counter. "Hey, you want to buy something?"

Bao has a super positive attitude, especially for a teenager.

He would totally be a member of the Vitakids gang. "Sure Bao," I say and buy a Diet Snapple for the ride home. While I pay, a six-foot customer in a yellow floral print dress enters the convenience store—yelling loudly at someone a few feet behind.

"You don't know how the fuck I do," she explains to her invisible companion. "Lord, it is a sauna out there."

I nod and wiped my forehead in agreement. She sashays over to the fridge. "What they even got to drink in here? I don't want no Gatorade."

I leave the store. From outside the door, I observe my student and his second patron of the afternoon. She is scanning the cigarettes behind Bao, straightening her platinum blonde bobbed wig.

"Hi Miss Loretta," Bao says.

"Well aren't you a polite young man," Loretta replies with small-town familiarity.

That's my cue. I did what I needed to do, saw what I needed to see, said what I needed to say. Tomorrow is another day and all that.

"See you in class, Bao." I pause. "And get some sleep tonight, will you?"

As I pedal out into Highland Avenue rush hour traffic, the sun sears the back of my neck—already burned by April in Los Angeles.

Acknowledgments

Coasting would not exist without the insights and critiques I received from my mentors, cohort, and teachers in the Antioch Los Angeles MFA program. My sincere thanks to all of you for encouraging me to write on. I also wish to thank my mother, Serl Zimmerman, for inspiring my return to school and always believing in my writing. Lastly, Adrienne, I will forever be grateful for your patience, brilliant input, and support while I turned these pieces into a book. This is for you.

A few of these stories were previously published, some in slightly different form. "Cure for Love" in *P.S. I Love You*; "It Couple" in *Entropy*; "Landmark" and "Gold Record" in *The Junction*; "Driving Dom" in *Literally Literary*.

About the Author

Ari Rosenschein is a Seattle-based author who grew up in the Bay Area. Books and records were a source of childhood solace, leading Ari to a teaching career and decades of writing, recording, and performing music. Along the way, he earned a Grammy shortlist spot, landed film and TV placements, and co-wrote the 2006 John Lennon Songwriting Contest Song of the Year. Ari holds an MFA in Creative Writing from Antioch Los Angeles, and his work appears in *Short Beasts*, *Drunk Monkeys*, *Noisey*, *Observer*, *PopMatters*, *The Big Takeover*, *KEXP*, and elsewhere. He lives with his wife and dogs and enjoys the woods, rain, and coffee of his region. *Coasting* is his debut collection.

You can connect with me on:

🌐 https://arirosenschein.com

📘 https://www.facebook.com/arirosenscheinauthor

🔗 https://www.instagram.com/arirosenschein

Subscribe to my newsletter:

✉ https://bit.ly/arimailinglist

9 798218 339968